Also by
MICHAEL LAWRENCE

The Poltergoose

THE KILLER UNDERPANTS

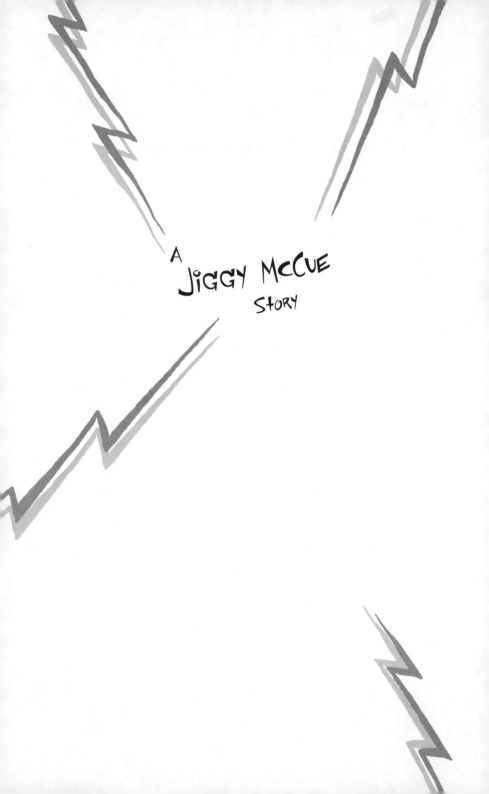

A JIGGY McCUE STORY

THE KILLER UNDERPANTS

by MICHAEL LAWRENCE

DUTTON

CHILDREN'S

BOOKS

New York

Text copyright © 2000 by Michael Lawrence

Library of Congress Cataloging-in-Publication Data
Lawrence, Michael.
The killer underpants: a Jiggy McCue story / by Michael Lawrence.—1st American ed.
p. cm.
Summary: Jiggy has a devil of a time with a new pair of underwear that refuses to be removed and which, when they start rippling and itching, cause strange things to happen.
ISBN 0-525-46897-8
[1. Underwear—Fiction. 2. Devil—Fiction. 3. Humorous stories.] I. Title.
PZ7.L43675 Ki 2002
[Fic]—dc21   2001047338

Published in the United States 2002 by Dutton Children's Books,
a division of Penguin Putnam Books for Young Readers
345 Hudson Street, New York, New York 10014
www.penguinputnam.com

Originally published in Great Britain 2000 by Orchard Books, London
Typography by Richard Amari
Printed in USA
First American Edition
2 4 6 8 10 9 7 5 3 1

This book is dedicated to Anthony Buckeridge,

whose tales of Jennings and Darbishire

were such a joy to me when I was Jiggy's age

THE KILLER UNDERPANTS

Before we go any further I'd better come clean about my underpants. What I mean is, no one actually died because of them—though there's no telling what would have happened if I'd had to wear them much longer.

I blame my mother. If my mom wasn't such a fanatic about the things you wear next to your skin, none of this would have happened. Okay, so maybe five weeks is a little long to walk around in a single pair of pants, but I always whip them off at night to give them a shot of oxygen, so what's the big deal? The morning my troubles started I'd just gotten out of bed and was slotting my trusty old snuggies into place for the day when Mom came in. Came in? She flung my door back so hard I almost went out the window.

"Jiggy McCue!" she screeched. "The state of your underpants!"

"Have you ever heard of knocking?" I said. "It's that little thing people do with their knuckles before barging into a kid's bedroom."

"They're disgusting," she said. "They're filthy. They're full of holes."

"Mother," I said, "they're supposed to have holes. Holes are what underpants do best. Now did you want something or did you just come in to trash my holey underpants?"

"I came in," she said, "because I'm sick to death of shouting myself hoarse for you to get up. But now that I've seen the condition of those articles, I'm going to have to reorganize my day. I have some shopping to do!"

"Oh no," I said. "Not new underpants. You know I hate new underpants. I've told you before, underpants need time to settle in, make themselves at home, breed a little friendly mold and fungus . . ."

I stopped. What was the point? She was a parent. Worse than that, she was a mother. Mothers don't understand these things. They also don't bother to listen half the time. "And you're coming with me," she said, to prove it.

"Whoa there," I said. "I don't do shopping, remember? Specially with my mother. It's number forty-seven in the *Book of Rules for Good Parents* I made for you and Dad at Christmas."

"Put something on over those hideous things, they make me feel ill," she said. "We leave in ten minutes."

"Wait!" I cried, skidding on my knees to my dresser. I tore a drawer open, started chucking things over my shoulder. "I have another pair, I know I have, saw them here only last month. Bingo!" I jumped up, shook my other cozy old pair of holey underpants in her face. "I'll just change into these, then we don't need to go and buy more—right?"

"Yes, you will change into them," she said. "Then I'll at least have the comfort of knowing that if you get knocked down by a bus you'll be in *clean* underwear."

"No, you miss the point," I said. "I mean I'll wear these *instead* of buying new ones. I'm saving you money. Why throw it away on new ones when I still have a spare pair? Okay, Mom? Deal?"

"No," she said. "Get changed. Now. We're going to the flea market."

And with those ten simple words my fate was sealed. The worst week of my life was about to begin.

2

No self-respecting kid wants to be seen shopping with his mother, right? Known fact. Why? Because when you're out shopping with the old dear you always, but always, bump into someone you know, usually just as she's patting your cheek or smoothing your hair down or something. My dad isn't crazy about shopping with Mom either, but at least she keeps her hands off his cheeks and hair.

"Why do I have to tag along?" Dad whined the Saturday morning she made us go to the market with her. "I don't need underpants."

"You need a new shirt," she said.

"No I don't. I've already got ten shirts for every day of the week."

She put on her Deeply Wounded expression. "Oh, so you don't like the shirts I buy you all of a sudden?"

He panicked. "No, no, Peg, you buy terrific shirts. But how many do you think a guy can get through in one lifetime?"

"That's the way I feel about underpants," I muttered.

My mother stuck her lip out and plunged after it into the flea market.

The market was pretty crowded. Half my class could be there. I had to keep my wits about me so I could jump away from my mother in a split second. It was okay being seen with Dad. With Dad you don't have to be on your best behavior, or look presentable, or tie your shoes, and he doesn't make you stand still while he holds bits of material against your chest to see if they match your eyes.

Well, there we are, Dad and me, slouching obediently behind the family tyrant, when someone from school comes along—not a kid, but almost as bad.

"Hello," said Ms. Weeks. "Joseph, isn't it? Joseph McCue?"

"No," I said.

"It isn't?" she said, surprised because she'd obviously gone to a lot of trouble to memorize the really smart kids' names.

"No, M'am, it's Jiggy, M'am. No one calls me Joseph."

"Why?" she said.

"Because all my life I could never keep still, ever since I was born—and before, according to my mom. She says I almost kicked her to a pulp before she even saw my face."

She smiled. "Jiggy it is then. And is this . . . Mr. McCue?"

Dad had stopped traipsing after Mom at the sound of Ms. Weeks's voice. Ms. Weeks has a nice voice, sort of soft and musical, and she has a nice smile and lots of blond hair, and when he got an eyeful of her my dad bounced back like a turbo-driven yo-yo.

"Call me Mel," he gushed. "Short for Melvin, terrible name I know, but I didn't choose it; there's Mel Gibson of course, though I'm taller than him; good weather we're having, how do you do?"

"*Dad!*" I hissed, laying a firm hand on his arm. Did I say it was okay to be seen with my father?

But Ms. Weeks wasn't fazed one bit. She just smiled in that nice way she has and stuck her mitt out. "Erica Weeks. New vice principal at Ranting Lane."

My ex-father went blank. "Vice principal?" He looked at the hand he was suddenly holding. "Ranting Lane?"

"Your son's school," Ms. Weeks reminded him.

"Oh, that Ranting Lane." My distant relative shuffled about bashfully, still holding her hand. "So *you're* the new . . . hm! Erica, you say?"

"Weeks. Just moved here with my mother." She glanced about. "She was with me a minute ago, I seem to have lost her."

"You can have mine," I said.

"Hello," my mother said, appearing out of thin air like an unbottled genie.

The complete stranger known as Dad threw Ms. Weeks's hand away and stuck both of his behind his back to prove they had nothing to do with him. "This is Emily Leeks," he said, "Jiggy's new price vincipal."

Ms. Weeks said hello to Mom but didn't stop to chat. "Must dash. If I don't track down my mother she'll get herself into trouble. Bit eccentric, you know."

Dad stood watching her go. "Nice, isn't she?" he said dreamily.

"For a price vincipal," Mom said. "We're in luck. I've found a stall that sells shirts, and right next to it there's a stall that sells underwear."

"Oh happy day," I said.

"And this time keep up," she said, and plunged back

into the throng. Dad jumped guiltily into line behind her and I got behind him, but not so close people would think I knew them. Then we set off once more on our quest for the underpants that were going to make me wish I'd never been born.

3

The stall that was about to turn my life into a nightmare looked like something out of a fairground. It was bright red with gold stars all over it and it had a big sign on top that said NEVILLE'S. It didn't take an Einstein to figure out that this was the name of the owner, a dumpy little man in a red bowler hat and yellow vest. He was a real grin-merchant, this Neville, but his grin was one of those insincere switch-on, switch-off types. The sort you buy in joke shops in a packet labeled "Bad Grin."

Mom made Dad stand still so she could hold a shirt against him from the stall next door. Then she told him to hold it there himself while she ransacked the underpants section of Neville's stall. Dad knew better than to move, so did the shirt, but I shoved my hands in my pockets to show how cool I was in case anyone saw me. While I hung there this little old biddy in a shawl hobbled by. She caught me giving her the cool once-over before I had a chance to glance elsewhere, and darted toward me.

"Lucky heather? Buy my lucky heather?"

I looked down my nose at this basket of purple stuff she'd stuck under it. "Heather?" I said. "What would I want heather for? I mean, like, what would I do with it?"

"Bring you luck," the ancient crone said. "Just a coin or two and good luck will follow you wherever you go. Don't you want good luck, young man?"

I chuckled, cucumber cool. "I make my own luck. Heather? Hey, who needs it?"

"That's a shame," she said. "Because great and terrible things are in store for you, and my heather might have protected you from the worst that is to come."

"Great and terrible things?" I flipped my collar up to cover the hairs that had just stood to attention on the back of my neck.

"I have the Eye," she said.

"Sorry to hear that," I said.

"Great and terrible things," she said again, and then once more, probably for luck: "Great and terrible things."

"Hey, this has been nice," I said. "Must do it again. Bye now."

"Beware the very next thing you touch," the little old woman said.

"I'll do that," I said, and turned away, laughing coolly.

"What do you think of these, Jiggy?" my mother said, thrusting something soft into my hands.

My laugh died. "Huh?"

"One hundred percent cotton jersey. Your size."

I looked down. I was holding this one hundred percent cotton jersey multicolored horror story against my lower decks.

"Mom. They're horrible."

"Well, we're getting them."

I looked up. It had to be better than looking down. Wrong. I stifled a shriek. My mother's eyes (which were glaring at me) were not their usual bluey gray color, they were all red and bulgy. I glanced round for the little old gypsy woman or whatever she was. She'd disappeared. Maybe before she went she'd passed the Eye on to my mother because I'd turned down her lousy lucky heather.

Mom turned to Neville the Badly Grinning Stallholder.

"We'll take these," she said.

I looked for my dad. A word from the Man of the House might help here, a second opinion that happened to be exactly the same as mine. The Man of the House wasn't there. He'd waited till my mother was concentrating on me, then dumped the shirt and made a run for it—to the nearest snack bar, knowing him.

"Mo-om," I said in a whiny little voice. It works sometimes. Not today though. She handed the money to Neville, and Neville turned the Bad Grin on me. I shrank back. The way he *looked* at me! Terrifying.

When we got home I was instructed to change into the new pants but take a shower first and get clean, Jiggy, *clean.* So I went to the bathroom, locked the door, turned the shower on, and sat on the toilet reading a comic till I felt enough time had passed. Then I flicked some water at the bath towel to prove I'd used it and unfolded the new underpants.

I didn't like them any better at second glance than at first. They had this swirly-whirly pattern all over them that made your head spin. Even the label was weird. It was on the outside, on the front—and *printed* backward. I didn't bother straining my brain trying to read the thing, but I made a vow to keep away from buses. Tire tracks might improve these things a little, but I wouldn't be caught dead in them, even to please my mother.

With a heavy sigh I stepped into the new underpants. Right foot, left foot, then the big upward haul, bend the knees for the last little lift, wriggle the hips to introduce them to the hardware, and there they were, home.

But then something happened. Something that doesn't usually happen when you put new undies on. They shrank to fit. Gave the personal places a sort of hello hug and forgot to let go. I felt like a cling-wrapped fruit bowl.

But it was at bedtime that I began to realize I had a problem on my hands. Well, not my hands exactly, but you know what I mean. I was stripping off to jump into my PJs and catch the fast train to Dreamworld, and everything went smoothly enough till I got down to the pants. They wouldn't budge. They absolutely refused to drop, or even droop, no matter how hard I tugged. My blinding new underpants with the dyslexic designer label clung to me like a second skin.

A second skin that wouldn't come off.

When I woke up the next morning I still couldn't get the new pants off, but at least they had the decency to open at the front a tad when my legs crossed, and let me drop them (but only just enough) when my eyebrows started to knit. Afterward though, like *immediately* afterward, they snapped right back into place and nothing would shift them till my next mad dash to the bathroom. It was as if they had a mind of their own, and that mind had made itself up that it'd found the boy of its dreams and didn't plan to leave him, ever.

I decided to inform the Golden Oldies that my underpants were holding me prisoner. Dad would have been first choice to tell because he can take almost anything, but he was out playing football with four other middle-aged hooligans and Dean from next door, which he does every Sunday morning because he's insane.

That left Mom. She should have been first choice really. She'd got me into this after all—into *them,* I should say. I'd heard her singing downstairs earlier, so the odds were she was in a better mood today. I put my bathrobe on and went down to the kitchen. She was loading the washing machine, which is one of those things she does really well. I tell her this all the time so she won't try and get me to do it.

"Mom, you know my new pants?"

"Yes, are they comfortable?"

"Well, there's sort of a problem. I can't seem to get them off."

"Now don't start that again, Jiggy. I want your pants changed daily, and that's all there is to it. That is, I will do once I get you some more. Can't think why I only bought the one pair. Silly really."

"But you don't understand," I said.

"Oh yes I do. Typical boy, you. Hate the idea of cleanliness. You wait till you start getting girlfriends."

I gripped the edge of something and closed my eyes. Why is it that conversations with your parents always swing wildly off course a heartbeat after they've started?

"Mom. Listen. Concentrate. The new hector protectors. They're stuck to me. I mean literally. As in superglue."

"Stuck to you? But you've hardly worn them."

"I thought it might be something in the material, like static."

"They should be all right," she said. "I know I got them from the flea market, but they weren't particularly cheap. Oh well, perhaps they'll work loose during the day. Don't forget to make your bed. I'm just slipping next door; Janet says she has some heather for me."

She opened the door and went out.

"Thanks for all the help and sympathy!" I called after her.

I decided to take advantage of my mother's absence and have a proper go at getting the new pants off. I draped my bathrobe over the bread box and stood there in my full glory: Underpants Man, scourge of sighted people everywhere. I looked around for inspiration. "Ah-ha," I cried, and sprang at the fish slicer.

Mom uses the stainless steel fish slicer for cooking bacon, eggs, sausages, fries, burgers and anything else you can think of except fish. I set to work easing the cold flat end into the band of my pants, just behind the stupid backward label. The plan was to get it right down inside, push the handle away from me, and loosen the pants just enough to slip them off.

That was the plan.

But as I tried to force the fish slicer inside, the band tightened. Tightened so much I had to lift my rib cage almost to the ceiling to grab some breath. I whipped the fish slicer out. The band loosened. I breathed properly again.*

Then I had another idea. You know the old joke about the person with the painful tooth who's too scared to go to the dentist? He loops a piece of string around the tooth, ties it to the door handle, slams the door and the tooth shoots out.

Well . . .

I managed to slip a piece of string through the flap at the front of the pants, the gusset, and work it up to the band on the inside. Then I looped it around and tied a good strong knot and tied the other end to the door handle. Finally I stretched out on the freezing cold phony quarry tiles and got set to give the door the good hard kick that would make it slam and whip my pants off.

* When I thought about it later, I thanked my lucky stars I gave up when I did. I mean that was one sharp fish slicer and I was shoving at it with all my might. I don't want to think about what might have happened if the band had suddenly let it in.

I raised my right leg, bent my knee, flexed my toes, took a deep breath. "One," I said. "Two," I said. "Thr—"

I stopped at "Thr" because my mother and Janet Overton from next door were suddenly standing in the doorway gaping at me.

I lowered my leg, slowly. "Hi."

Mom and Mrs. O. just stood there holding these plant pots and feasting their eyes. My mother's eyes were bright red and almost popping out of her head, the way they'd been at the market. Janet's were brown, and shrinking rapidly to the size of raisins because she wasn't used to coming into neighbors' houses and finding the son and heir flat out on the vinyl with his gusset tied to a door handle.

"Jiggy, what . . ." Mom inquired in this strangely quiet voice, "what are you doing?"

"Testing the handle," I replied, quick as a ferret. "Thought someone should find out how strong it is. And you know what? It's terrific. I'd say we have a real winner here."

I know when I'm on a losing streak. It's a gift I have. I needed help. The help of quick young minds like my own. It was time to call in the Musketeers. I got dressed and crossed the road. It seemed wise to do it in that order.

Pete Garrett and Angie Mint's house is pretty much like mine except theirs doesn't have a stone gnome in the backyard and the towels are different. Pete and Angie aren't related, but they live under the same roof these days because Pete's dad and Angie's mom moved in together and the kids had to go somewhere.

"I have a problem," I said when we were sitting in a circle of three on the floor of Pete's bedroom.

"Join the club," Pete said.

"Why, what's your problem?"

"I haven't got one," he said.

"But you said join the club."

"So?"

I let it go. Sometimes talking to Pete is like talking to Stallone, our cat. No, that's not fair. Stallone would be insulted.

"So what is it?" Angie said.

"What's what?" I said.

"Your problem."

"Well, it's . . ." I began, and stopped because a funny thing had happened.

I'd come over all bashful.

Now you have to understand that Angie and Pete and I have known one another since year one. We used to hang side by side in a row from our mothers' chests while they talked about last night's TV programs. In our youth we swapped half-sucked M&M's and stood on our heads in puddles together. When we were seven or eight we discussed the really important things, like how far you can fire balls of snot with an elastic band, and does the president have his own private toilet, stuff like that. In other words we were close. But this, well. Heavy. I don't know why it didn't occur to me before I crossed the road.

"No offense, Ange, but this is man talk."

"It's what?" she said.

"Sorta personal. Not for the ears of mixed company."

"Since when were we mixed company? I thought we were best buds, the Three Musketeers, one for all and all for lunch."

"We are," I said. "Always have been, always will be, but will you leave the room please?"

Angie jumped up. She was really angry.

"I get the message. Last place I want to be is somewhere I'm not *wanted*."

She stalked to the door and slammed it behind her. There was a pause, then another slam as she went into her room along the landing. Pete and I sat in a circle of two, not looking at each other. It was a tense moment. Neither of us had ever asked Angie to leave us alone before.

But then Angie put on a CD and turned the volume to full and we stopped being able to hear ourselves think, which broke the tension a little. I yelled my problem at Pete and he yelled his advice back, which was to go home and close my eyes so that when I woke up I'd realize this conversation was all a stupid dream.

There was a sudden hammering at the door, which we could just about hear over the music.

"YEAH?" Pete hollered.

The door didn't open. The hammering came again, louder.

"COME IN!"

It still didn't open, and the next lot of hammering almost brought it down on top of us.

Pete got up. *"Are you DEAF?"* he shouted.

He grabbed the handle. Yanked the door back. Angie stood there looking so mad I threw my arms over my face.

"IS IT MY FAULT I'M NOT A BOY?" she screamed, and stormed back to her room. Her door slammed again.

Pete closed his door, quietly. He said something.

"WHAT?" I yelled over the music.

He started to repeat it but changed his mind, reached for a scrap of paper and a felt-tip. He wrote something and shoved it at me.

Maybe you ought to tell her, the note said.

I took the felt-tip and wrote: *Would you tell a girl if you had a problem with your underpants?*

Pete read this and took his pen back. The music stopped suddenly as he was writing. He handed me the note.

She's not exactly a girl, it said. *She's Ange.*

I turned the paper over and wrote: *It's still embarrassing.*

He wrote: *Yeah, well.*

I wrote: *Why are we still writing when it's gone all quiet?*

He wrote: *Beats me.*

"Stay here," I said, with my voice.

"Right," he said, with his.

I left the room. On the landing Angie's mother, Audrey, was just leaving Angie's room. "And keep it *down!*" she said into the room. "Hello, Jig," she said to me, and went downstairs.

I stood in the doorway she'd left open. Angie was sitting on the bed, fists clenched, scowling at the carpet.

"Can I come in?" I said.

"No," she said.

I went in. "Can I sit down?"

"No," she said.

I sat down. "You can hit me if you like."

"I wouldn't soil my hands," she said.

"No, go on, hit me, you'll feel better."

She thumped my shoulder with a fist like a rock. Right on my booster shot. My nose hit the carpet.

"Man talk!" she snarled at me.

I lay on the floor holding my shoulder. I knew without checking that she'd knocked the scab off. Still, there'd be another one along soon, I could pick at that.

"I wasn't thinking," I said, getting to my knees. "Fact is, I need your help, Ange."

"Well, why don't you ask *Pete* then?" she said bitterly.

"I did." I got off my knees. "Should have known better."

There was a shy little knock on the open door. "All buds again?" Pete said.

I looked at Angie. "Buds again?"

"Only if we don't have secrets."

"Deal."

I held my hand out. She hesitated, but then held hers out too. "One for all and all for lunch," we said as we did the secret handshake. I'd tell you about the secret handshake but then it wouldn't be secret anymore, so forget it.

I told her what I'd yelled to Pete, about the pants that wouldn't let me take them off. I even told her about the fish slicer, though I skipped the string and door handle tragedy. I'd just about finished and was about to ask her what she thought I ought to do, when Pete said:

"Underpants."

"Er, yes," I said, "that is the topic of the day."

"I was just wondering why they're called that," he said. "I mean, why underpants?"

"Why is a house called 'a house'? Why is milk called 'milk'? Why are you called 'airhead'?"

"No, I mean why 'underpants'? Why not 'under*pant*'? I mean it's only one thing, right, like a shirt? You don't say a pair of shirts, do you?"

"You might if you had two," I said, "and they matched."

"You couldn't have a pair of underpant," Angie said. "Sounds stupid."

"Yeah, but that's what I'm saying," Pete said. "It shouldn't be a pair of underpant, it should be *an* under-pant, like *a* shirt."

"It's probably to do with the number of legholes," said Ange. "Two legholes equals pants. One leghole might equal pant, but then where would you put the other leg?"

"A shirt has two armholes," Pete pointed out.

"That's true," said Angie.

"Heavy stuff," said Pete.

"Yeah," said Angie.

"Excuse me," I said. "Fascinating as all this is, it's not getting us much closer to solving the biggest problem of my life so far."

"What problem's that?" said Pete.

I thumped him. Right on his booster shot.

Of course I should have known that Angie would ask to *see* the pants under discussion. She wouldn't be Angie if she didn't. Pete laughed cruelly, made himself at home in her rocking chair, rolled up his sleeve, and got to work on his loose scab with a fingernail.

"But I'm still wearing them," I said to her. "That's the problem."

"So lose the jeans, I don't have telescopic vision."

"X-ray," said Pete, picking and rocking, rocking and picking.

"Oh, I don't know about that," I said.

She put her hands on her hips. "Jiggy McCue, do I have to remind you that I've seen you without your diaper?"

"Not recently you haven't," I said.

"Yeah, well I can still picture everything if I try *really* hard."

She screwed her eyes up and got down to some serious picturing. I covered my zipper.

"But what if your mom comes back and I'm standing here in my underwear, what then?"

"We tell her the truth. We say you're showing us these new pants you're so thrilled with."

"That isn't the truth."

"She won't know that. Strip!"

I unzipped.

"Do you want the music back on?" Pete said.

"Shut up."

My jeans hit my ankles. Pete's smirk hit his ears.

"Wow," said Angie. "Don't you have to have a license for things like that?" She meant my pants.

She strolled round me a few times. I stared at a spot on the wall. Pete rocked and picked and smirked, back and forth, forth and back, rocking, picking, smirking.

"Writing on the label's backward," said Angie.

"Probably made in Hong Kong," I said.

"Show me how you can't get them off."

"How do I do that?"

"You try to remove them, and fail."

"What if it works this time?"

"Then you don't have a problem after all."

I wasn't sure about this. "Look away just in case?" I pleaded.

"But then I'll miss it," she said. "Whichever way it goes."

I shuffled round, jeans hugging my ankles, till I had my back to her. Then I tried to hook my thumbs in the waistband of my underpants. The band tightened, trapped my thumbs, squeezed hard. My rib cage rose.

"If this is the audition for Grandson of Tarzan," said Pete, "all I can say is: next!"

The band loosened a little. I dropped my ribs, welcomed my thumbs back with open hands.

"See?" I said to Ange.

"See what? All I saw was you pressing your thumbs into your waistband and sticking your sad little chest out."

"Okay then," I said.

I gripped the looser material just below the equator and tugged southward. The pants clung to me like a pancake to a ceiling.

"Let me have a go," Angie said, reaching for me.

"Get off!" I said.

She dropped her hands. "You're doing it again."

"Doing what?"

"Being sexist. I bet if it was Pete trying to pull your pants down you wouldn't object."

"I can't believe you just said that."

"Look, let's stop messing around," she said. "If they come away in my hands I'll close my eyes, I promise."

This wasn't a decision to be made lightly, so I sighed heavily before making it. "All right, but watch where you grip or I'm calling my lawyer."

She walked around me a couple more times like an explorer looking for the source of the Nile. "There's more slack at the back," she said, and grabbed me from behind.

I squealed.

She regripped (the material this time) and tugged. No movement. She tugged again, harder. This time the pants moved, but took me with them. She had another go. Same thing.

In the next few minutes Angie swung my pants around the room several times, with me still in them. I was getting pretty tired of smacking the wall with my palms by the time she finally let go and said: "Know something, Jig?"

"What?"

"You've got a problem."

It was about here that I felt a ripple. In my pants. I didn't realize it till later, but this was a sign of stuff to come, like a warning.

"Hey," I said.

"Hey what?" said Ange.

"My pants are moving."

We stood there watching them ripple. It started at the front, then moved around, like a breeze whipping across a lake. Felt weird, but it was a definite improvement on being hugged to death.

But suddenly the ripple died. And the itch started. An itch like no other in the noble history of itching. An itch that ran around inside the one hundred percent cotton jersey like an angry rat in a cage. I went after it, scratching like I'd been to evening classes in Advanced Scratching and wanted a diploma. At first Pete and Angie didn't pay much attention, thinking it was just me living up to my name, jigging around the way I do when I get agitated, or when music starts, or when I'm given homework, or—well, you name it. They got more interested when I ran at the dresser, though, and started rubbing my underpants area up and down and side to side against the edge.

"Bears do that," Pete said.

"Rub themselves against dressers?" I replied, arms in the air, hips swaying, jeans around my ankles. "I don't think so."

"Against trees. But I bet if you gave them a dresser they'd be very grateful. They could also store their fur coats in it on hot days."

"Pete," I said, "will you do me a favor?"

"Name it, Jig." He chortled.

"Go flush your head down the toilet."

He stopped chortling, jumped up, flicked his scab at the wall, ran out of the room.

"Was it something I said?" I quipped merrily as I rubbed up against the dresser, trying not to think of bears.

Angie went to the door, leaned out. "He went to the bathroom," she said.

"Terrific," I said.

I rubbed some more. The itching was easing off. I started to look forward to sighing with relief.

"He just flushed the toilet," said Ange.

"Good news," I said.

I continued rubbing myself against the dresser till I was sure my pants were an itch-free zone once more.

Pete returned. He looked a little dazed. He also looked a little wet above the neck, and there were streaks on his cheeks. Blue streaks that dripped on to his shoulders and spread slowly across his chest.

"I just flushed my head down the toilet."

"Is that something you do a lot of in your spare time?" Angie asked.

"Jiggy told me to," he said, dripping bluely. "He said flush your head down the toilet and I went straight to the bathroom, got down on my knees, stuck my head in, and flushed. Couldn't help myself. There was this new bowl freshener thing in there too."

"I don't get it," I said. "I mean, I didn't hypnotize you or anything. I wouldn't know how or I'd have got you to do that years ago."

"Maybe your itchy pants had something to do with it," Angie said.

"How do you mean?"

"Well, you started scratching just before you told Pete to flush his head. Bit of a coincidence. Hey, wouldn't it be a laugh if when they get itchy and you scratch, people have to do whatever you say?"

"Yeah, that would be a laugh," I said, not laughing.

Just then I caught a glimpse of myself in the closet mirror. Even with my jeans around my ankles it was an impressive sight. But there was something else. I shunted closer for a better look. In the glass, the letters on the backward label weren't backward.

"Holy underpants," I said.

While Pete dabbed at the blue streaks on his shirt with a curtain, Angie joined me at the mirror. We stood side by side reading my label the right way around. Reversed in the mirror, the backward letters made real words. These:

LITTLE DEVILS

7

The next day was Monday. It usually is after Sunday. Monday afternoons we have soccer with Rice. Chicken with rice would have pleased me more, but nobody asked me when they wrote the menu. Mr. Rice is our gym teacher and he wears this stupid red jogging suit all the time. I mean he even wears it in *assembly,* which is pretty sad. Soccer is my most hated sport in the universe. I could never understand what people see in it. Nor could Pete at first. We started this antisoccer club when we were about eight but only two people joined—us—and after a while even Pete canceled his membership and started kicking a ball about.

The girls are lucky. They don't have Mr. Rice for outdoor sports, they have Ms. Weeks. This really irritates Angie. Not that she wants Rice or his lessons. It's the discrimination that gets up her nose. "Why do we have to do field hockey and softball?" she asked Ms. Weeks one day, just after Ms. Weeks started. "Why can't we play football and regular baseball and stuff?"

"Because you're a girl, Angela," Ms. Weeks replied.

"Don't rub it in!" Angie snapped, and stomped off.

Another thing Angie hates is having to put on this weeny little skirt that shows her undies. I don't blame her, so would I. Ms. Weeks wears the same outfit when she takes the girls, weeny little skirt, bright green undies. The boys find this quite interesting. I mean how often do you get to see a teacher's undies? I'll tell you. Every Monday afternoon at Ranting Lane School.

Anyway, there are the girls and Ms. Weeks on that side of the field, jumping in the air and showing their green undies, and here are the boys on this side, kicking stupid balls about, and suddenly old Rice Cake is bellowing at me from across the field.

"McCue! You're goalie!"

Rice always bellows. The only time his sentences don't end in exclamation marks is when he's talking to Ms. Weeks. Then you can hardly hear him with an ear trumpet.

"Goalie?" I yelled back. "Me? You have to be kidding, sir!"

He put his head down and charged across the field fingering his whistle. The man in red never goes anywhere without his whistle and is always blowing it to make you jump. As he came at me I started wishing I had a personal hero to hide behind. Mr. Rice is about twice as tall as anyone else in the school, with these shoulders like ox thighs and a jaw like a set square, and he scowls a lot, and when he's really annoyed his forehead throbs and veins stand out in his neck. They were standing out now.

"What was that?" he barked as he approached.

"What was what?" I replied.

He stood looking down at me. "What did you just *say*, boy?!"

I stood looking up at him. "I said, 'What was what,' sir."

"I mean *before* that!"

"Dunno, sir, can't remember."

"I'll tell you what you said, sir! You said 'You have to be kidding, sir,' that's what you *said*, sir! Now get in that goal or see me after showers! Ryan, make yourself useful somewhere else! Hey, you two! Hegarty! Sprinz!"

Hegarty and Sprinz were mud-wrestling in a puddle. While Rice shot off to pull them apart, Bryan Ryan sauntered out of the goal so I could saunter in. He gave me this superior half-amused look that said, *You're gonna regret taking my job, McCue.* Soccer with Mr. Rice is the highlight of Ryan's feebleminded week.

As this was soccer practice, not actual soccer, the idea was that we all did a bit of everything so we could learn to be soccer stars if we failed at everything else. Now that I was goalie, Mr. Rice planned to make the most of my terrific skill and interest. He told everyone to stand in a line facing me. The first six all had a ball at their feet. Ryan was one of them. Mr. Rice blew his whistle and the first ball came toward me. I raised my arms and jumped to the far right. The ball bounced in at knee height to the far left.

"Is that the best you can do, boy?!" Rice screamed.

"Just about," I said, wheezing a bit.

"Well, try harder or you'll be over there with the girls!"

"I'll go now if you like, sir."

"Stay where you are! And block goals!"

The next ball came right at me. I ducked just in time. It sank into the net behind me.

"The idea is to *stop* it, McCue, not get out of its way!"

"Really? Hey, didn't know that, sir."

Another ball came. This time, to show I was willing, I flicked a finger in its general direction as it passed.

"McCue, you are *useless!*"

"I'm quite good at art!" I yelled back.

"Ryan! Do your stuff!"

Ryan grinned, flexed his elbows, spun around, and trotted so far up the field that I began to think he was going to the movies. But then, when he was down to a dot on the horizon, he turned around, jogged in place for a minute because he knows how impressed we all are by jogging in place, and finally set off at a run toward the ball. I was not terrifically excited about this. In ten seconds that ball would be zooming at me with enough speed to lay out an African elephant, and there I was with no choice but to stand with my hands on my waist waiting for it.

Ryan was forty feet away and closing when I felt a ripple. I looked down. My gym shorts, which I was wearing over my new underpants, were on the move. I tried poking at them. The ripple moved on. I followed it. Same result.

"What the hell are you doing *now*, McCue?!" roared Mr. Rice.

I might have answered, but suddenly the ripple stopped and I had more important things on my mind. It began with a little tickle somewhere too private to mention and spread through my pants like chicken pox on ice until, just as Ryan's boot connected with the ball, I fell to the ground scratching like a maniac.

"McCue, you *twit*!" I heard as the ball slammed into the back of the net—slammed so hard it bounced back and hit me between the shoulder blades. Any other time I might have been a tad upset about this, but a soccer ball in the back was nothing compared to the misery of the mighty Itch. I writhed in the mud, stuck my legs in the air, then my back end, then jumped up to rub myself raw against the goalpost.

Mr. Rice jogged up. "What are you *playing* at, McCue?! I know you have trouble keeping still sometimes, but this is *ridiculous!*"

I threw myself across his enormous sneakers. I wriggled between them. I got on all fours to scratch against his leg like a dog against a lamppost. He bawled something from on high, don't ask me what, I wasn't listening. I replied with the first thing that came into my head, which I also didn't listen to. This was not the time for a heavy chat with a jerk in red. But then something weird happened. The moment I said whatever it was, my favorite sporty type spun around and bolted across the field. I didn't call him back. I missed his leg, but at least I could get down to some serious writhing and scratching without being shouted at.

After a while the itching eased off and I was able to focus on bits of the outside world. The bit that most appealed to me contained a long red streak running round the field at breakneck speed. Mr. Rice. And he wasn't only running. He would run for about fifteen feet then jump in the air, run fifteen feet, jump in the air, run fifteen feet, and so on. Somewhere in all this his whistle must have got stuck in his mouth and started paying rent, because every time he jumped it gave a little shriek. So what we had now was run-jump-whistle, run-jump-whistle, run-jump-whistle, all around the field. Everyone stopped what they were doing to watch, including Ms. Weeks and the girls. Some of the boys cheered him on. Creeps.

Pete joined me as my torment shuddered to an end.

"What's old Rice Pudding up to?"

"Must have finally boiled over," I said, getting to my feet.

Mr. Rice started to slow down. Now he was only jumping every nine feet and not quite as high. Even his whistle was a whisper of its former self.

"Jig," Pete said, "you were itching just now, weren't you?"

"Just a bit," I said.

"Did you say anything to Rice?"

"I might have, dunno, I was sort of distracted."

"You can't remember what?"

"Does it matter?"

"It might. Remember me sticking my head down the toilet?"

"Oh. Yeah. See what you mean."

"So try and remember what you said."

I didn't have to try very hard. It came back all of a sudden, like an unwanted boomerang between the eyes. I gulped. Cleared my throat.

"What?" said Pete.

"I told him," I said, "to go take a running jump."

8

I'm sure Mr. Rice had no idea what had made him do the running-jumping-whistling stunt around the field, but he needed someone to blame, and who better than the last person he spoke to before doing it? When he finally came to a halt he advanced on me, puffing hard, muttering my name over and over with exclamation points. So eager was he to get his hands on me that he didn't notice Ms. Weeks coming up behind him bouncing a ball, followed by her girls.

"Mr. Rice, that was very impressive."

Rice froze, forehead throbbing, neck so knotted it looked like it needed a surgical collar. He heard the words before realizing who said them and you could almost see him thinking, *Someone's pulling my stupid leg here.* But then he recognized the voice and his neck and forehead stopped throbbing, his jaw went slack, he turned around—and instantly became Quasimodo with neck-to-ankle blushes.

"I've never seen anyone run and jump so fast," Ms. Weeks said, bouncing her ball. "What a marvelous example for the boys!"

Mr. Rice glazed over, just like my dad when he met her at the market. It's just as well she doesn't have that effect on the boys or we'd get even less work done than we do already.

"You must be very fit," Ms. W. went on, for his ears and mine alone.

Rice moved his lips around silently, reached for a soccer ball to bounce in time with hers. In a dreamy sort of bark he told me and the others to go and get in the showers, and Ms. Weeks told the girls to do the same, but different showers, and we all ran off, leaving the two of them alone in the middle of the field, gazing into each other's eyes, bouncing their balls in perfect rhythm.

Showers. Now tell me, why is it that boys have to shower together and girls don't? At our school anyway. I mean, Angie Mint might feel she's being discriminated against because she has to do girlie sports and stuff, but at least the girls get separate shower stalls. Not us.

Oh no, we have to all pile in together and look as if we enjoy it. Why? Are we not human too? Pete manages to get out of showers. He put this note together on his computer. It's got Dr. Wolfe's letterhead and Dr. Wolfe's forged signature and Dr. Wolfe saying he must be excused because he has veronicas or something. Works like a charm. Wish I'd thought of it.

I had a special reason for not wanting to shower in public that day though. So I hung back, fiddling with the muddy knot that always seeems to get into my laces, till the others had stripped off and raced one another into the steam, screaming at the top of their voices. Then I kicked my boots off and started to get dressed.

And guess who trotted in.

"What's this, McCue, done already?! Impossible. Your hair should be wet if nothing else is!"

Before I could think of a decent lie, a squeaky little voice piped up from behind a locker door.

"McCue didn't go in yet, sir."

I glared at the weed as he flashed by, shoulder blades like traffic cones, rear end like matching pickle jar lids.

"Thanks, Skinner! Do the same for you sometime!"

"Get in there, boy!" Rice bellowed at me. "And no buts!"

"No butts in the showers?" I said. "How does that work?"

By the time I was down to my underpants Rice was in his little office next to the changing room, probably doing something sporty like replacing the worn pea in his whistle. I walked slowly to the showers, took a deep breath at the door, and ran in, hoping the steam was dense enough to hide the one hundred percent cotton jersey multicolored horror story glued to my beauty spots. I might have got away with it if I hadn't slipped on a bar of soap and said "Yump!" as I hit the tiles. The crowd in the showers stopped kickboxing empty air and running up and down flicking bare parts with wet towels. As I got up, thirty eyes peered through the steam in disbelief.

"Waheeey! Look at McCue!"

"Ya godda death wish or somethin', Jig? Rice'll murder ya."

"Better you than me, pal. You're dead."

I grinned around like I knew what I was doing and stuck my head under a vacant shower while they got it out of their system. In a minute or two they'd scattered again. All except one. Eejit Atkins.

"Atkins," I said gently, "why are you sharing my shower?"

"Admirin' ya pants," he said out of the side of his mouth.* "Whereja geddum?"

I looked down, amazed. "You *like* them?"

"Yeah. Cool."

"If I could get 'em off," I said, remembering to talk out of the side of my mouth, "you could have 'em, free gift, no strings, no refunds. There's no one I'd rather give them to—'cept maybe Ryan." I winked at Bry-Ry, who did not wink back. "Or Rice," I added, for my own pleasure.

"Or Rice what, McCue?!" boomed my hero from the doorway.

"*Nice,* sir," I replied. "I was saying how nice it is here. In these showers. At this school. With these teachers."

"Do my eyes deceive me?!" Rice said, hardly able to believe what they'd just picked out through the steam. "When I say get in the showers, boy, I mean get in them *naked*! I do not mean get in them dressed for *bed*!"

---

* Atkins always talks out of the side of his mouth, unless he's talking to teachers or his mom. He thinks it's tough. Some of us talk back to him out of the side of our mouths so he won't feel stupid.

I glanced down at myself and slapped my forehead. "Silly me. Must have slipped my mind."

Eejit Atkins sidled off and I closed my eyes to listen to the water hammering on the top of my head. Good beat. My feet started to move, fingers clicking wetly.

"WHAT DO YOU THINK YOU'RE DOING, McCUE?!"

I peeped through my dripping lashes. Even through the steam I could see a throb starting on Rice's forehead.

"I'm taking a shower like you told me to."

"WITHOUT THE *UNDIES,* BOY! WITHOUT THE *UNDIES!*"

"He's shy, sir," Ryan said. "Doesn't want us to see him without his willy warmers. Come on, McCue, get 'em off!"

There was a pause while the others considered these fine words, decided they liked the sound of them, and started repeating them.

"Get 'em off, get 'em off, get 'em off!"

"Get 'em off, get 'em off, get 'em off!"

"Get 'em off, get 'em off, get 'em off!"

"QUIIIIIYUUUUUUT!!!" screamed Mr. Rice.

The chanting stopped. The only sound was a tile falling off the wall, and the hiss of the showers as Mr. Rice stepped down from the doorway. He stood at the far end, water lapping his sneakers, eyes like penlights with my name on them.

"I don't know what your game is, McCue, but I want those things off! Now! Instantly!"

"No can do, sir," I said. "Sorry, but there you are."

"WHAT?!"

"I would if I could, and that's the truth. I'd gladly stand here without my pants looking as pathetic as everyone else, but I can't. They won't let me. The pants, I mean. Seems to be something in the material, and I don't mean me."

He started toward me without the slightest concern that fierce jets of water were trained on him from both sides and that water makes you wet. Boys parted before him like the Red Sea before Moses. Next thing I know I'm being gripped by the bicep and lugged across the tiles with one shoulder on a level with the top of my head, the other trailing along behind like an unwanted relative.

Then we're out in the chilly changing room and Rice is plonking me down on a bench. As the water from my pants patters through the slats into someone else's shoes, he leans down and puts his nose against mine.

"You know, McCue, when I was a kid the gym teacher would take his tennis racket to a boy for so much as walking out of step! But this is the twenty-first century and I'm obliged to be nice to you instead of giving you the thrashing you deserve! So I'm going to ask you— very nicely, very politely—to run ten complete laps around the sports field every morning before homeroom for the next two weeks! That all right with you, *Mr.* McCue?!"

"Which way, sir?"

"What do you mean, which way?!"

"Around the field. Or will you leave it up to me?"

"For that, boy—twenty laps!"

"Great," I said. "Nice round figure. I can do ten each way."

This must have satisfied him because he unstuck his nose from mine, jerked up to his full height, where birds flew, and stalked out leaving a trail of colossal footprints in case anyone wanted to follow him. I dried my feet on Ryan's towel. I wasn't bothered about Rice's punishment because I had no intention of doing it. No one does Rice's punishments. They don't do them because by the next day he's always forgotten he's given them. Something to do with all the balls he's head-blocked in his prehistoric life is my bet. Damaged his sporty little brain. Mr. Rice has the shortest memory since . . .

Sorry, what was I saying?

It was just as well gym was the last period of the afternoon, because it isn't all that comfortable walking
around in wet briefs under your pants. Also, wet patches
have a way of appearing in all the wrong places, which
means that people call their friends and point at you. So
after school I ran on home, ahead of Pete and Angie. I
went around the back as I always do after school and
was approaching the gate when one of our next-door
neighbors stepped out of his. This was Dean.

Dean and his girlfriend, Pearl, moved in a couple of
days after we did. Couple of nights actually. One day
the house was empty, the next they were over borrow-
ing sugar, coffee, milk, cereals, bread, baked beans, and
a comforter. Pearl & Dean are quite young, in their
twenties, and they have these three huge black dogs
called Chico, Harpo, and Groucho, but no curtains.

Mom says curtains are expensive. Dad says they'd be able to afford curtains if they stopped feeding the rotten dogs. My dad doesn't like dogs. He thinks Dean's okay, though, probably because he's also a football nut. Dean is one of the fanatics that get together with Dad on a Sunday morning, and the only one that isn't middle-aged. He doesn't look much like the others either, because they don't have rings in their eyebrows and gold studs in their chins and shave their heads. Mom used to shudder whenever she saw Dean, which annoyed Dad. "So he likes jewelry," he said. "Well, so do you. So he shaves his head. I shave my jaw, you shave your legs and armpits, each to his own."

"Ma man!" said Dean as he closed his gate.

He held up his palm. I slapped it. Then I held mine up and he slapped it. Then we did a little something with our wrists and threw our thumbs over our shoulders.

"See ya 'roun', man," Dean said, and bounced off waggling his elbows to the music inside his little bald head.

I opened my gate and went up the path. There's never any problem getting in the house when the Golden Oldies are out at work, you just stick a finger in the garden gnome's bottom. My father won this gnome in a raffle. He was thrilled senseless because he never won anything before. He thought it should earn its keep, though, so he introduced the gnome's posterior to his faulty power drill. When he'd finished he sat back proudly and said, "Well, how many burglars do you know who'd think of looking up a gnome's butt for the back-door key?"

Neither Mom nor I had the heart to tell the poor old wacko that burglars don't usually bother with keys, wherever you hide them.

First thing I did when I got in was go upstairs and kick off my damp pants. Then I tried a hopeful tug at the Little Devils to see if the water had loosened their grip. They shrank. Dramatically. I gasped. Stopped tugging. They relaxed.

I plugged in my mother's hair dryer and prayed that they didn't have any objection to being dry. I turned it on, aimed, held my breath. No, they didn't seem to mind.

"Hi, Jig."

I dropped the hair dryer. It turned itself off. Dad stood in the doorway.

"What are you doing here?" I demanded.

"I live here. I'm your father."

"But you should be at work!"

"Afternoon off," he said.

"Well, next time clank your chains or something so I'll hear you."

He grinned at the hair dryer on the floor and the underpants on me. "I used to do that."

I gawped. "You had underpants that wouldn't come off too?"

"No, I just used to do that." He left the room.

I picked up the hair dryer and clicked the switch a few times. Nothing happened. I pulled the plug out and put it back again, clicked the switch a few more times. Still nothing. I wound the cord around the dryer and put it back in Mom's cupboard. She could fix it. She's a wiz at stuff like that.

Monday evenings my old lady goes to her French class at the Adult Education Center. Dad went there for a couple of weeks once. Not to learn French, though—for a drawing class. A Life Drawing Class. He was pretty disgusted when the "life" turned out to be a bowl of flowers. Mom's more dedicated. She's been learning French for about half my life. Her French teacher is this woman called

Francine, from New York. Francine has the heaviest Brooklyn accent you ever heard. "How do you know she's not teaching you to speak French with a Brooklyn accent?" Dad asked after Francine came over to our house one time. This really annoyed Mom, who says that Dad never misses a chance to ridicule the stuff she does. Mom can't wait to try out her French in France, she's always saying so. And at last she's going to get her chance. She's arranged this romantic long weekend in Paris for one. She asked Dad to go with her, but he said, "What, are you crazy? It's the middle of football season."

Anyway, Monday evening, Mom at French class, me and Dad in the living room. I was trying to do some homework on the dining room table and Dad was watching football on TV, and the yelling was starting to get to me so much I had to ask him to control himself. I'm a great disappointment to my father. When I was born he bought me a rattle to celebrate. Not a neat little rattle in blue plastic from Mothercare that makes a nice gentle sound when you shake it, but a huge wooden noisemaker that people down to their last brain cell whirl around their heads at football games. Maybe that rattle's why I didn't follow in Dad's football steps. It terrified me.

While my father did raving lunatic impressions in front of the TV, I stared at the sheet my math teacher had handed out. At the top of the page it said: *Draw quadrilaterals (four lines) around the following pairs of diagonals.* I wondered what for. Was this something you did a lot of as an adult? If not, why waste time learning how to do it at school? I mean isn't there something more useful they can teach us, like how to keep spaghetti on a fork, how to watch the stuff on cable that your parents don't want you to, how to get your underpants off?

"Dad," I said.

He didn't answer. His eyes were pasted on the screen, where all these loonies in shoulder pads were throwing their arms around one another and patting one another's behinds.

I said it again, louder. He glanced at me as if I'd just strolled into church with a whoopee cushion. "Dad, I can't remember the difference between a rhombus and a trapezium."

"What?" he said.

I repeated this too.

"Rhombus," he said. "Roman fella. Had a twin. Big on wolves."

"Father, this is math."

"Oh, right." His eyes darted back to the shoulder-pad brigade, probably to see if they were exchanging boxes of candy yet and going for walks together and taking turns with the dishes. "What was the other one?"

"Trapezium," I said, without much hope.

"Roman again," he said. "Some sort of arena. Or maybe something to do with a circus. Trapeze, see. The word is the key. Maybe even a Roman circus. That fit?"

"Yeah, great, Dad. Don't know why I didn't think of it myself."

"You only have to ask, Jig, only have to ask."

We returned to our separate worlds for a while. Then he started shouting again, bouncing up and down on the couch with his hands in his armpits. "Did you see that? Did you *see* that? A fumble like that would have had him thrown to the Christians in Nero's time!"

I shook my head sadly, wondering if anyone has ever done any research to see if there's a link between the ways of ancient Rome and barbarians stomping around muddy fields wearing numbers and hugging one another. I made no comment, but a few minutes later there was a deafening roar from the TV and my unbalanced father jumped off the couch and ran around the room punching the ceiling. I sighed and gathered up my books.

I was halfway up the stairs when the phone rang. Dad didn't hear, so I got it. It was Pete and Angie. The idle chitchat lasted about three and a quarter seconds before we got to the Little Devils and the Itch and how people had to do what I told them to when I was scratching.

"What worries me," I said, "is what I do if the Itch comes on in class."

"You try not to scratch it," Angie said.

"Impossible. The Itch *demands* to be scratched. No way out."

"You start scratching in class," Pete said, "and I ask to be excused in a hurry."

"Correction," said Angie. "If Jiggy starts scratching in class, *he* asks to be excused in a hurry. Then he races off to the Boys' Room, bolts himself into a stall, and stays there till he either stops itching or gets so thin he falls in and drowns."

"I can't go to the Boys' Room," I said. "Someone might come in. Those stalls don't have roofs, and the doors have these colossal gaps at the top and bottom, so if I speak the person's bound to hear me even if he can't see me."

"So keep your trap shut."

"Don't know if I can."

"Yeah, you always did have a problem with that," said Pete.

"I mean imagine," I said, "if I can make old Sugar Ricicles do my bidding, anything can happen. I mean, like . . . *anything.*"

"Hey, that's right." Pete again. "You could tell him to take a stroll off a cliff." There was a pause while Ange and I listened to his mind clank. "Think of it. This great red monster kicking and screaming all the way down. We could take pictures."

"It would be murder," I said. "I'd be a murderer."

"Killer McCue," said Pete. "I can see the wanted posters now."

"Wouldn't be your fault," said Ange. "When they haul you in front of the jury you blame your underpants. They wouldn't believe you, but . . ."

"Yeah," said Pete, still on his theme. "This huge great poster nailed to trees: WANTED. DEAD OR ALIVE. KILLER UNDERPANTS."

And that's how they got their name really.

10

I met Pete and Angie outside their house as usual the next morning and we set off for school like on any normal day. Except that it wasn't a normal day. Normal days were a thing of the past for me.

Ranting Lane is a big school, with hundreds of kids who have to change classrooms every period, like musical chairs without the music. This is so the teachers don't wear their poor old feet out coming to us. There are no lockers to stash our things in, so several times a day we have to trail around this enormous building with our coats and sports gear and backpacks full of everything but the taps from the kitchen sink. Carrying this heavy stuff around all the time means that everyone walks with one hand trailing on the ground, even on the way to school. This is rough on kids like Eejit Atkins, who like to walk with both hands on the ground, on account of their having only just dropped down from the trees.

"Well, if it ain't the three Muskiteers."

Atkins backed into our path from the bus shelter he'd been decorating with a spray can. We walked around him. He caught up with us, fell in step, dragging a hand.

"You hear the news?" he said out of the side of his mouth.

"What news?" I said out of the side of mine.

"We're movin'."

"Movin'?" said Pete out of the side of his mouth.

"Yeah. We're bein' rehoused."

"Rehoused?" said Angie out of the side of her mouth. "Where?"

"Your estate," said Atkins with a happy laugh, and loped off to bond with some idiot buds.

"Atkins moving to the Brook Farm Estate?" Pete said in horror, forgetting not to talk out of the side of his mouth.

"This is not good news," I said, remembering.

"Understatement of the millennium," Angie said. "Atkins as a neighbor is the nightmare scenario to end all nightmare scenarios."

I ought to tell you that Eejit and his older brother, Jolyon, and their parents live at the end of Borderline Way, the street where Pete and Angie and I lived all our lives till we moved to the estate. Jolyon Atkins used to build trash-can barriers across the road and charge kids to get in and out. Some of the parents too. Jolyon's a big kid, with a barbed-wire tattoo where his collar should be. Even his old man has to watch his step with Jolyon. Eejit isn't so bad, but he really looks up to Jolyon and just loves the barbed-wire neck. There's no one at home on Planet Eejit.

Anyway, the story was this. The Town Council was going to pull down Borderline Way house by house, starting with the Atkins's because it's almost a ruin already thanks to the boys. That part was okay. What wasn't okay was that they'd promised them a house on our sparkling new estate.

"Mr. and Mrs. Atkins are all right," said Angie, searching for the bright side.

"Yeah," I said. "Quite normal really."

"Snag is that where they go, Jolyon and Eejit go."

"Yeah," I said. "Major snag."

"Trevor Fisher says they could move on the weekend," said Pete. "He should know, his dad's on the council."

Angie forgot the bright side. "The weekend? *Next* weekend?"

64

Pete nodded.

"Well, that's it then," she said. "By Tuesday there'll be graffiti on the lampposts and beer cans in the bushes. Six months from now the Brook Farm Estate will be a brand-new slum."

"Still, could be worse," I said.

She stared at me in disbelief. "It *could*?"

"Sure. Loads worse. I mean, wherever the council puts them, it won't be near us. Every house on our street's taken. There's a family in every one, and sometimes a dog and a hamster."

"The people next door to us have cockatoos," said Pete.

"Painful," I said.

"Yes, there is that," said Angie.

"There is what?" said Pete.

"Like Jig says, Eejit and Jolyon can't move onto our street. With any luck we'll never see them."

"Yeah," said Pete. "It'll be okay."

"Yeah," said I. "Be fine."

We nodded silently together at this comforting thought. Yep, things could be worse.

We were right.

They could.

A whoooooole lot worse.

I was nervous all morning about what might happen next with the Killer Underpants. So nervous I couldn't concentrate on my classes. That's my story anyway. But the Itch didn't come, and at lunchtime I started to relax a little.

There's this place at Ranting Lane called the Concrete Garden where Pete and Angie and I eat our lunch most days. There are classrooms on three sides and these little concrete pigeons all over the place and a tree that isn't concrete. We have our own private bench where we swap sandwiches. Pete likes the sardine-and-tomato-paste ones my mother makes for me every day of my life and I prefer his cheese and lettuce, which he doesn't like, and quite often we trade with Angie for her sandwich spreads because they make her throw up. That way we're all happy, even our parents who don't know they're making sandwiches for the wrong kids.

"Geography next," I said gloomily, feeding the lettuce from one of Pete's sandwiches to a concrete pigeon.

"Only an hour," said Angie.

"A lot can happen in an hour. I could get the Itch and start giving orders all over the place and the school could be in smoking ruins by the end of the lesson."

"And the downside of that is . . . ?"

"Hey," Pete said suddenly, "did you hear about the Olympic swimmer who set out to swim across this colossal lake?"

"What colossal lake?" I said.

"It doesn't matter what colossal lake, this is a joke."

"Pete, one thing I do not need right now is jokes. Especially yours."

"Yeah, well this Olympic swimmer was three quarters of the way over this colossal lake when he started to get tired and knew he couldn't make it. So what do you think he did?"

"He drowned?"

"No. He swam back again."

I tore my bag of chips apart with my teeth. I was about to dip in when I noticed something that made me groan with despair.

"Oh no! She's given me sour cream and onion now! I hate sour cream and onion! I want regular! I'm always telling her, don't experiment on me, I say, don't try things out on me, regular, that's all I want, regular, is that so hard to understand? That woman has got to go."

I offered the bag round. "Trade?"

They turned their backs and stuffed decent chips into their chipholes, leaving mine to hang there watering.

Near our bench there's this little fishpond. After a hard morning at the desk it soothes the nerves to sit there watching those big goldfish weave in and out of all that weed trying to find their way home.

"I envy them," I said.

"Envy the fish?" said Pete. "You want gills? You want pop eyes? You want to be painted gold and have fins and a tail?"

"They don't have underpants problems."

"They wouldn't, they don't have anything to put in them."

"Nice peaceful life swimming around all day, eating what they like when they want, no one bothering them."

"No lousy lessons," said Angie.

"No itching and scratching," I said.

"Scratch and sniff," said Pete.

Angie and I looked at him under our eyebrows. You never know what's coming next with Pete.

"Your underpants," he explained. "They're like those scratch-and-sniff cards."

"Scratch and *sniff*?" said Ange, pursing her lips. "His *underpants*?"

"Sort of. 'Cept they're scratch and speak. He scratches, he speaks, people do what he says."

I patted him on the head. "Thank you, Pete. Eat my lunch like a good boy." I worry about him sometimes.

Just then I felt something in my pants.

"Uh-oh," I said.

"What's up?" said Ange.

"I'm rippling. Means the Itch is coming."

"See ya!" said Pete, throwing his chips in the air and disappearing in a puff of salt.

Angie stayed put. She always was made of sterner stuff than him.

"Jig! Quick! To the bathroom!"

"It's lunchtime!" I said. "It'll be full of heavy smokers!"

"Well, here's their big chance to give up. You order them to."

"Here it comes!" I started to scratch. "Oooooooooh! Agony! Murder!"

Angie put her chips down and edged away, proving

that the stuff she's made of isn't *that* much sterner than Pete's.

"Don't say a word!" she said.

"I'll try," I said, scratching two-handed.

"I said not a *word!*"

I leapt off the bench and fell to my knees in order to rub my backside against the concrete pigeon I'd just put on a low-fat diet.

"Ange," I said.

She slammed her hands over her ears and high-tailed it. "I can't hear you," she said as she followed Pete out of sight. "Can't hear you, can't hear you, can't hear you, can't hear you!"

I grabbed a fistful of her abandoned chips and stuffed them in my mouth. At least one good thing had come out of this.

"Never get tired of playing the fool, do you, McCue?"

Bryan Ryan stood looking down at me from the steps of the classroom he'd been doing a detention in. There were many things I wasn't in the mood for just then, and Ryan was pretty near the top of the list.

"Take a walk, Ryan," I said.

But then I had a thought.

A thought and a half.

"Yeah, Bry-Ry, take a walk. In the fishpond. Eat weed!"

I didn't have to say it twice. Ryan dropped his backpack, gym bag, and lunch box, and jumped into the fishpond. Splish, splash, splosh. He reached down. Goldfish swam for their lives as he grabbed their weed.

The Itch was starting to fade as Pete's and Angie's heads poked around a wall to see if it was safe to return. They saw what Ryan was doing. Saw him shoving slimy fish weed between his teeth, gulping it down, stuffing more in by the handful.

"You have anything to do with that?" Pete asked me.

I stood up, dusted myself down, shrugged modestly.

"Now that's evil," said Angie. "That is pure *evil*."

Ryan suddenly lost interest in his latest food fad. He looked up from the water. His eyes were a little on the wild side. He had all this green stuff hanging from his mouth, like a vegetarian vampire. He did not look happy.

First thing I did when I got home was strip off in my room and go to the mirror on the wall. The time had come for a heavy talk with my underpants, man to gusset. Okay, so I'd had a bit of fun with old Ryan, but next time I might not be thinking when I spoke. Next time I might do some innocent bystander some serious damage.

"Now let's get a few thing straight here, Little Devils," I said sternly. "You're very smart, I'll give you that. You can make people do stuff and you have a wicked sense of humor. Consider me your biggest fan. But listen, you are not a higher life-form like me. You are what the higher life-form wears around his privates to stop the world from calling the cops. I say what goes, not you. I mean, yeah, you might be one hundred percent cotton jersey, but I'm one hundred percent flesh, blood, bone, and toenails, so no contest. Now speaking as a higher life-form to a lower one, I'm going to tell you what you have to do. You have to stop ruining my life. Got that? Has that penetrated? Do I make myself clear?"

I suppose it's too much to expect a pair of underpants to fall to your ankles and beg forgiveness, especially underpants with a mind of their own, but personally I think they overreacted a little when they shrank to about half their normal size, which made them suddenly so tight there was only one thing to do.

Stand on tiptoe and scream.

A few minutes later when they'd loosened enough for me to wipe the tears from my eyes, I noticed in the mirror that the backward letters on the Little Devils label had changed. Now the label read:

YOU WERE SAYING?

"I was saying," I said wearily, "that you are the superior being. Number one big cheese. The underpants-that-must-be-obeyed-without-question-at-all-times. El Bosso."

The letters changed again. This time they said:

BETTER BELIEVE IT KID

12

I needed a day off school. Apart from the fact that school was a dangerous place to be right now, tomorrow was Wednesday; midweek flea market day. The bozo who sold the underpants to my mother might be there again. Maybe he knew what they were capable of. Better still, maybe he could tell me how to get the darn things off.

But you can't take time off school just because you've got better things to do. No, you have to pretend it's something else. Like illness.

"Think I'll go to bed," I said in a faint voice halfway through dinner.

"Bed?" Mom said. "But it's fried chicken. Fried chicken is your favorite. You're always saying how you love fried chicken."

"Feel weird," I said.

"In what way?" she demanded.

"Kind of weak. And I keep getting dizzy. And there's this pain in my chest. And I'm all hot and cold at the same time."

"Sounds like·me when my team loses," said Dad.

"Well, you go and get a good night's rest," said Mom. To me, not Dad.

"I'll try," I said with a small cough that said I can't promise anything, and plodded upstairs with lead in my slippers.

When I was in bed I played music very quietly till it got dark. Then I played it some more until I heard M & D coming up. I turned the music off just in time. The door opened, ever so quietly.

"You asleep, Jiggy?"

I said nothing. Made no move.

She closed the door, ever so quietly.

I waited while they took turns in the bathroom, turned off the landing light, got into their creaky old bed. Then I waited for my mother's book to hit the floor. Her bedtime reading always falls out of her hand after ten minutes because reading in bed makes her nod off. She's been on the same book for ten months. It's a thriller.

Their lights went out. The house was dark and silent.

I waited for two more minutes before sitting up in bed. Then I let go a terrible cry of pain, thudded out of my room and along the landing, and slammed the bathroom door loud enough to wake the next street but one. Then I gave this almighty roar like a werewolf ripping a sheep apart, and another as a second sheep strolled by, and finally raised my voice in a wail of misery so tragic that the heartstrings of a charging rhino would have been plucked.

Then I flushed the toilet and waited for reactions.

There weren't any.

Not a sound, not a whisper, not the patter of a single tiny foot.

I opened the bathroom door.

"Mo-om?" I called feebly.

Nothing.

"Da-ad?"

Nothing.

I dragged my poor old carcass to their door and looked in, expecting their bed to be empty because they'd climbed out the window and gone to a nightclub on the sly. But they were still there. Snoring.

I went back to bed.

. . .

To get things rolling in the morning, I didn't get up when Mom called me. Then I didn't get up when Dad called me. Then I ignored the bell. When Mom can't get an answer from me on a school day she shakes this brass handbell she keeps on a little table at the bottom of the stairs. Drives me up the wall.

"Jiggy, you'll be late for school!"

"Errrrgggggh," I said.

"Are you all right?" she yelled.

"Oooooooooooh," I replied.

She came up. I'd been rubbing my eyes to make them all swollen and my hair was all over the place and I'd wrecked the comforter and pillows. When my mother came in she found me lying with one hand trailing on the floor like a dying poet, swollen eyes trying bravely to open, lips doing their best to smile at her and croak something heroic.

"Jiggy, what *is* the matter?"

"Uuuuuuurrrrrrrrrrrggggggh," I said.

She felt the forehead I'd just scraped on the carpet for a minute or two.

"You're burning up," she said.

"Waaaaa-ter," I gasped. "Waaaaa-ter."

"You want some water?"

"Essss . . . pleeeeease."

She went out to the landing and shouted down. "Mel, get me a glass of water for Jiggy, he's not well!"

I heard Dad mumble something in the distance and Mom repeated the order, then came back to soothe my fevered brow and say coochie-coo things like, "There, there, it's all right, Angel, Mommy's here," like I was suddenly half my age.

Dad hauled himself upstairs and came in with half a glass of water, and Mom asked him why only half a glass, and he said, "Tripped on a stair, what's the matter with him?"

I groaned and Mom gripped my neck in the crook of her arm and poured water into me. I let it trickle down my chin and rolled my eyes in case she'd missed how swollen they were.

"I was so sick in the night," I whispered huskily.

"Well, why didn't you *call* me?" she cried, horrified to think of her little one hanging over the toilet without her standing there pointlessly patting his back.

"Didn't want to . . . disturb you."

She gave my shoulders a squeeze to show how touched she was. I winced bravely. And then she said the magic words.

"Well, you can't go to school like this."

"This takes me back," Dad said.

"What does?" said Mom.

"I used to come over all peculiar when I wanted a day off school."

Mom was disgusted. "Mel, how could you even *think* that? It's quite obvious he's sickening for something."

"Oh, he's sickening all right," Dad said, and scooted downstairs, whistling heartlessly.

My wonderful mother gazed at me with big worried eyes. "I don't like to think of you lying here like this all day with no one to look after you. Perhaps I ought to take a day off wo—"

I jerked into a sitting position. "NO!" I yelled, so loud she jumped out of her slippers. Then I remembered I was sickening and fell back again.

"Well, if you're sure," she said, patting her heart. "But I'll bring you some breakfast on a tray."

"I couldn't eat a thing," I said pathetically.

"You must try, darling. You must keep your strength up."

"No really, Mom. You go to work. I'll be all right after a day in bed, I'm sure I—*cough, cough*—will."

She hesitated, but gave in. "I'll leave the curtains closed so you can get some sleep, okay?"

"Thanks, Mom."

She gave me a sad sympathetic smile and went to the door, where she stood for a count of five hundred wearing a last lingering look of tragic love, and left me to it. Half an hour later she and Dad went off to work. Thirty seconds after that I was stuffing spare pillows under my comforter to make it look like I was fast asleep if anyone came back and looked in on me without an appointment. Then I got dressed and went downstairs, filled my pockets with cookies, and slipped out the back way in my dead grandfather's baseball cap so no one would think I was a kid taking a break from school.

13

The Wednesday market wasn't as crowded as the Saturday market, which meant I had to keep my head well under the hat. I wished I'd thought to pencil in a mustache to make me look older, but even a genius can't think of everything. The bright red stall with the gold stars was there again, and so was the chubby little man called Neville, in his red bowler and yellow vest. He was still grinning his big joke-shop grin when anyone looked his way and still losing it the moment they looked away. I wasn't sure which I preferred, Neville grinning or Neville not grinning. Either way, he didn't look like the sort of man you walked up to and asked for an antidote to your underpants.

"Excuse me. My mother bought some underpants from you last Saturday."

The grin evaporated. "You gotta complaint? Take it someplace else, I'm a busy man."

"No," I said, "no complaint, it's just . . . well, yes," I said, "I do have a complaint actually. I can't get them off. And they make me . . . itch."

"Heeeeeey . . ." said Neville, suddenly interested. "Are you the one who got the pants with the snappy design?"

"Snappy design?" Well, maybe it was all in the eye of the beholder, and his eye was blind. "Yeah, that's me."

"And they stick to you like glue?" he said.

My pulse started to race. "Yes! That's right! I've been wearing them for four days and nights, nonstop."

"And they make you itch, you say?"

"Itch? I never would've believed such itches were possible."

"And what do you do about it?" he asked.

"I scratch. I have to. Like a lunatic."

Neville tugged his bowler over his eyes and leaned closer. "When you scratch, do you . . . say anything?"

I tugged the baseball cap over my eyes and also leaned closer. "Yes!" Oh, he understood everything! I would have kissed him if he wasn't so ugly. "And whatever I say *happens*! Like if I'm itching and scratching and I say to someone jump through that window, you know what? They jump. Have to. No choice, true as I stand here."

Neville drew back. That great unjoyous grin surfed across his chops.

"Gooood!" he said.

"What?" I said.

"They work!" he said.

"What do?" I said.

"The pants!" he said.

"You mean all that is *meant* to happen?" I said.

"You betcha!" he said.

"But it's *hell*!" I said.

"Fine place!" he said.

I didn't seem to be getting anywhere.

"Has anyone else bought pants like mine?" I asked him.

"No, just you. Nobody else seems to like them."

"*I* don't like them," I said. "Trouble is I'm stuck with them. Literally."

"Be philosophical," he said cheerfully. "In those pants, for the price of a small itch, you can make every one dance to your tune."

"I don't have a tune," I said. "All I want is to get them off. Come on, please, there has to be a way."

"Nope. Once you step into a pair of my Little Devils they're with you for life—yours or theirs, whichever lasts longest. That is, unless they come in contact with . . ."

He deliberately didn't finish the sentence and winked at me.

"Come in contact with what?" I said.

He tapped the side of his nose. "Trade secret."

I suddenly became all weak. "Why are you doing this to me?"

"Don't take it personal," he said. "It could have been anyone."

"Anyone whose mother is feebleminded enough to buy your rotten underpants."

"So blame your old lady. Did I force her to buy them? Did you see me twisting her arm? I think not."

"Who are you, anyway? How can you make things like this happen?"

He flipped a business card out of his vest pocket. Handed it to me. I read it.

"Ever hear of a dude called Lucifer?" he said.

"Lucifer? You mean . . . ?"

Neville nodded. "My big brother. Started out with a bit of a complex, old Luce. The other kids called him Lucy. So he decided to stir things up a little. Did pretty well for a time. Too well. Burned himself out. Now it's my turn."

"Your turn?"

"Yep. Neville the Devil's time has come. I'm setting up on my own."

"With underpants?"

"I'm starting at the bottom."

"So it's your mission in life to make mischief?" I said. "Create havoc? For the fun of it?"

His grin reached the back of his neck. "Couldn't have put it better myself. But a good devil has to keep his eye on the market, and seeing as no one else has your mother's fine taste in underwear, starting Saturday I'm switching to saucepans, frying pans, cheese graters, stuff like that. Soon I'll have Little Devil utensils in half the kitchens in the country. Might even launch my own website."

"What mischief can a cheese grater get up to?" I asked.

Neville the Devil's grin came a little unstuck at the edges. His eyes became shifty. "I'll think of something."

Realizing that I'd get nothing out of Neville the Devil I returned sadly to the Brook Farm Estate, opened my back gate, headed up the path.

And found someone in the yard, kneeling over the rock garden.

Some*thing.*

"Jiggy!" the red-faced, bug-eyed monster cried when it saw me. "But . . . but you're upstairs! In bed!"

"Er . . ." I said.

The monster got off its knees. I thought it was going to rush me and tear out my spleen, whatever that is, and I got ready to make a run for it.

"I was so worried about you I came home from work," the creature said. "I went up to look in on you. You were asleep, so I thought I'd plant the heather Janet gave me. And all the time . . . all the time . . ."

"I just popped out for some air," I said. "Thought it'd

make me feel better. Mom," I said, for it was she, "what's wrong with your face?"

"My face?"

"Yes, it's sort of . . . horrible."

She went into the house in a kind of daze, still trying to make sense of me not being where she'd thought I was, and found a mirror. If this had been Hollywood her scream would have won an Oscar.

After catching me up and about when I should have been groaning under the comforter, nothing could persuade my mother that I was really ill, even when I had a dizzy spell and fell facedown on the couch before her bulging red eyes. She said next time she'd listen to my father, who obviously had more experience with lying and shilly-shallying than she did. She grounded me for the rest of the week (which unfortunately didn't include from school) and phoned Dad at work to tell him to come home because she thought she must have caught some fatal disease and wanted to share it with him. When Dad came in he yelped and flew back against the door. Then he bundled her into the car, wearing gloves so he wouldn't have to touch her, and drove her to the doc's by the nonscenic route.

"So what's wrong with her?" Pete asked later, as we

hung around my backyard. (I was allowed as far as the fence, and my friends could still come over.)

"Dr. Wolfe says she's probably allergic to heather." I crooked an elbow in the direction of the garden. "Mom was planting it just before she turned into Alien 10."

Angie wandered over to the heather. "Doesn't look like much of a threat."

I followed her. "It's probably not the heather. That doctor's a quack. Never gets it right with me."

"That's because there's never anything *wrong* with you," said Pete, joining us at the heather. "Nothing a mail-order psychiatrist couldn't sort out. Lucifer's little brother! Tee-hee-hee."

I sighed. He'd been like this ever since I told him and Angie about the trip to the market. Even when I produced Neville the Devil's business card Pete thought I'd been suckered.

"Hup!" I said suddenly.

Angie narrowed her eyes at me. "Hup?"

My hips gave a jerk, all by themselves. Angie looked down. So did Pete. So did I. Something was moving in the South Pole region. My lifelong buds stepped away from me.

"Wait," I said. "It's different this time."

"Tell us later," said Pete, backing down the path. "Over the phone."

"It's weird," I said. "Not like the ripple I get before the Big Itch. It's like . . . it's like the pants are having a hard time of it all of a sudden. Like they're, well, not feeling so good."

"Aw, poor things," Pete said, keeping his distance.

"Jig," said Angie thoughtfully, "remember the doc said your mom could be allergic to heather . . . ?"

"Yeah, so?"

"Well . . ." She nodded at the purple stuff we were standing over.

"You don't think . . . ?" I said.

"You never know."

"What?" said Pete from along the path.

I squatted beside the heather. The underpants fluttered frantically like there was a giant moth trapped inside them instead of just me.

"Why didn't I think of it before?" I said.

"You didn't think of it this time," said Ange.

"Remember the little old gypsy type at the market?"

"No," said the other two Musketeers.

"No, that's right, you weren't there. Well, last Saturday, just before my mom bought the Killer Underpants, this gypsy woman tried to offload some lucky heather on me. Naturally I gave her the thumbs down, but then she said . . . she said . . . what was it now . . . ?" I rubbed my fevered temples with my fevered knuckles. Then I had it, word for word. "She said, 'Great and terrible things are in store for you, and my heather might have protected you from the worst that is to come.'"

"Another loon," said Pete. "The market must be full of them."

"Maybe. But my underpants have just gone slack."

"That must be nice."

"You have no idea." I stood up. "And Neville dropped a hint that they might be beaten if they came into contact with something. He wouldn't say what, but my guess is it's heather."

"So if you'd bought heather from the old gypsy type," Angie said, "you might never have had all this trouble."

"Right," I said. I glanced toward the house. I could hear the TV. The Golden Oldies were watching it to take their minds off Mom's face. "Ange, look away."

"What for?"

"Gonna take my jeans off."

"So?"

I didn't want to go through all that again. I took my jeans off and rubbed heather between my palms and patted my underpants all over. Almost at once I felt something sort of like a gasp deep within them.

I plucked at the band. And it let me! I looked down. For the first time in four days there was a gap between the band and me. I'd never seen anything so beautiful. Angie stretched her neck to look too.

"Get outta here!" I said, and let the band snap back.

"All right, I will," she said and stalked off down the path in a huff. Slammed the gate behind her.

"She's very touchy these days," I said to Pete.

"Women," he said.

"Don't let her hear you say that."

I got down on the heather, stretched out, started rolling about in it, back and front, front and back, ditto, ditto, hoping the stuff would sap the strength of my pants. Pete left. I guess it's not much fun watching someone roll around in heather.

In a while I stood up in the heather to check how things were going down below. The front flap was opening and closing like a vertical mouth gasping for air. I thumbed the band of the pants, tried a little downward tug. They budged.

"Yes!" I said, and tugged again.

They budged a bit more, but stuck at half-mast. Still, half-mast was a definite improvement over full-mast, and the front flap was opening and closing quite frantically now.

"Jiggy! What are you *doing*?!"

I turned around. My mother stood in the patio doorway. I pulled my pants up, the last direction I wanted them to go, and stepped away from the heather. The waistband tightened. The front flap snapped shut.

"What have you done to my heather?" Mom said.

Her eyes were almost back in her head by this time and her face was just a ripe peach sort of color, but she didn't look like she planned on coming any closer just in case Dr. Wolfe knew what he was talking about for a change.

"I rolled on it," I said, and aimed a pair of irresistible cow eyes at her. "To teach it a lesson for what it did to my mom."

She resisted. "You *rolled* on my heather? In your *underpants*?"

"Didn't want to get my jeans dirty."

She ordered me upstairs to wash the garden off my magnificent torso and legs. I used her towel. In spite of everything I wasn't sorry I'd taken the day off. For one thing I hadn't had the Big Itch all day. For another I'd learned that the Killer Underpants could be defeated— by heather. Even by the ordinary nongypsy nonlucky variety from next door.

I went to my room lighter of heart than I'd been all week. But I'd hardly got through the door when I felt a tug at my gusset. Then it was pulling me across the room. It stopped pulling when I reached the mirror. I stood watching the letters on the backward label regroup. The words they became brought me crashing back to earth with an incredibly dull thud.

YOU'LL PAY FOR THAT

But I was in a good mood again the next morning. I knew what I had to do to defeat the Killer Underpants. After school I was going to spend the entire hour and a half before my parents came home rolling in Mom's heather. All right, so I'd be grounded for the rest of my life, but it'd be worth it. When Pete and Angie and I set off for school I was singing quietly under my breath. I didn't even grumble when Pete asked me why honey is so scarce in Brazil.

"Dunno, Pete," I beamed. "Why is honey so scarce in Brazil?"

"Because there's only one 'r' in Brazil," he said, and cracked up.

"Er, shouldn't that be only one 'b'?" I said.

"It was 'b' the first three thousand times I heard it," said Ange.

Pete stopped cracking up. "What do you mean, only one 'b'?"

"The reason honey's so scarce in Brazil. Because there's only one bee in Brazil."

"Yeah, but there's also only one 'r,'" he pointed out.

"In that case I don't get it," I said.

"Me neither," said Ange.

"No," Pete said. "Nor did I when Eejit Atkins told it to me."

The first lesson of the day was PE with my old pal Mr. Rice, which would have been a good reason for taking a second day off if I could have gotten away with it. I just can't see the point of PE. I mean, like, why do we need to learn how to jump over a horse, specially one that looks nothing like a horse? Why do we have to lie on the floor and pass beanbags to one another with our feet? Why run around the gym handing a stick to one another when we could stand in a small group and do it without getting out of breath? The only thing that makes sense in any of this is the name of the lesson: Pointless Exercises.

Next up, though, was art and design, and I don't mind that. Mr. Lubelski takes us for A & D and he's Polish, from Poland, and nice. Today we were drawing feet. That is, half of us were. The other half, the ones with a bare foot each on chairs, were sitting back with their hands behind their heads, criticizing. There was one major drawback to this lesson. Mr. Lubelski had provided the chairs to put the feet on but he hadn't thought of providing pegs for our noses. I was drawing one of Pete's feet and I almost passed out just looking at it. The nails were rimmed with black, jagged as a rusty chain saw, and you could have hit the dirt between his toes with an arrow from the far end of the sports field. As for the smell, think cheese factory, double it, multiply it by four hundred, then ram your nose into a block of ice to stop it from self-destructing.

"Jiggy," Mr. Lubelski said in his nice accent, "do you really need to wear pencils in your nostrils?"

"Only way to survive, sir."

He wandered over half smiling, but when he got close I saw him go all pale and grip an easel. "I see what you mean," he said, and tottered to the window for a portion of air.

Pete scowled. "Get a move on. I don't want to sit here all day having my foot pulled to pieces."

"Best thing for it," said Angie from six feet away.

It was when Mr. Lubelski was called away on school business that the day went all wrong. I was sitting there quietly drawing Pete's foot and Pete was sitting there quietly moaning while all hell broke loose around us. "I mean what is the point," he was saying, "of being left in a classroom without a teacher if you don't pile chairs on top of someone, rub everything off the blackboard, and hide the teacher's briefcase?"

"Sit still," I said. "I'm just getting the hang of that toenail."

"Which one?"

"The black and green one with the walrus mustache. Hup!"

"Hup?" he said suspiciously.

The pencils dropped out of my nose. My underpants were rippling. Rippling like never before. Rippling so hard my pants might have been full of bubbles.

"Is it what I think it is?" Pete said.

"Could be," I said, and hit the ground scratching.

Pete's chair did a double somersault as he jumped to his foot. The class cheered. They thought we were fooling around. Copycat chair somersaults followed. Desks flew. From the floor where I was writhing I saw Pete dodging falling furniture, knocking over art materials, plunging through bundles of kids as he made for the door.

And a terrible idea came to me. I mean a really awful

idea. An idea so disgusting and cruel that if I hadn't been rolling around the floor scratching like there was no tomorrow I would have been sitting in a straitjacket hugging myself with glee.

To put my brilliant idea into action I needed a victim. I wasn't fussy, anyone would do. I grabbed the nearest ankle. Tugged at it. The owner of the ankle came tumbling down on top of me. I pushed him off. He rolled on his side. Faced me. It was Ryan.

Bry-Ry had been keeping his distance ever since the fish weed incident. Like Mr. Rice after his running-jumping-whistling stunt, I don't think he understood what had happened, and because he was Ryan he didn't believe for a minute that he'd done something I'd told him to, but he kept giving me these wild looks, half fearful, half vengeful. And now we were lying nose to nose on the floor of the art room.

"You did that on purpose, McCue!"

No, I thought, I can't do it to him again—can I? And then I thought: Yeah, course I can! I grabbed his ear. "Wipe every trace of dirt off Garrett's foot, Ryan," I whispered into it. "With your *tongue!*"

Oh boy, was this gonna be good!

"You're out of your tiny mind," Ryan said.

I stared at him through a haze of frantic scratching. Why hadn't he jumped up and gone after Pete? Always worked before, and this time I really *wanted* it to work. I mean, like, *really* wanted it to work.

Ryan got up and gave me an affectionate kick in the ribs that I hardly noticed. I glanced around from worm level. Pete had stopped near the door to see what happened, pretty certain now he wasn't near me that it would be someone else who got dumped on. Little did he know it, but he wasn't off the hook yet. Someone had his beady eye on him. Someone who had to wipe that foul foot clean with his tongue if it was the last thing he did.

Me. Jiggy McCue.

The Killer Underpants had said they'd make me pay, and they'd meant it. I was going to have to carry out *my own orders!*

Pete must have realized something was wrong when I started slithering across the floor toward him, because he spun around and lurched at the door. He didn't make it. I grabbed him by the heel. By the bare, nauseatingly unclean heel.

And licked it.

"Huh?" Pete said over his shoulder.

Maybe because he was so shocked, maybe because I had his foot in my mitt, he tottered and went crashing over.

His foot was even more hideous up close. Smeared with all kinds of filth, dotted with grit, fluff, slimy stuff, and—I swear on my cat's life—a squashed spider. And I had no choice but to wipe it all off. With my tongue. I got to work.

"HUH?!"

This was the rest of the class. They'd stopped trying to wreck the room. They stared in horror as . . .

I won't describe it if you don't mind. My stomach heaves just at the thought of it. I was still itching like crazy, but my need to lick the dirt off Pete's revolting foot beat even my need to scratch myself senseless. It was my most miserable experience ever and I couldn't stop. Pete yelled and squealed, twisted and tugged, but I had him in a foot lock. Nothing he did could free his foot from my grasp or keep it from my dirt-hungry tongue. I had superhuman strength. I was a kid possessed. By Killer Underpants.

But then, as suddenly as it had come over me, the need to poison myself left me. At the same moment I realized I wasn't itching anymore. I jumped up, rushed to the big white sink in the corner, and spat and spat and spat. Then I drank a jar of dirty paint water and spat and spat and spat some more. I might have gone on doing this for some time if Pete hadn't lugged me away by the neck and shoved his licked foot in the sink and attacked it with the big wire scrubbing brush, going "Eerk, eerk, eerk," and shuddering so hard it's a wonder his shoulders didn't fall off. He didn't mind his feet being absolutely utterly out-of-this-world repulsive, but he got plain ill at the thought of it being wet-cleaned by human tongue. I understand this.

16

Pete wasn't all that keen on sitting next to me for the rest of the day. He gave the impression that even sitting in the same galaxy was a bit of a problem. He wasn't very happy about walking home with me after school either come to that, and kept ten paces behind all the way. Once again Angie showed that she was made of sterner stuff. She walked just five paces behind.

"You can't blame *me,* Pete," I said, strolling backward. "You think I *wanted* to lick your lousy foot? You think it's my *wish* to die horribly from the Black Death? Come on, man."

"Did I hear a little voice?" Pete said, scanning the sky. "The voice of someone I never want to see or speak to again?"

"Yep," said Ange, from five paces in front of him.

I protested. "It's the Little Devils! They said they'd pay

me back for heathering them, and they did. They turned everything around, made *me* do what I told *Ryan* to do!"

"Did the same little voice of someone who no longer exists as far as I'm concerned," Pete said to the sky, "did it just say that it told *Ryan* to lick my foot?"

"Yep," said Ange.

"And does this person who is now totally extinct actually expect me to *forgive* him?" Pete said.

"Yep," said Ange.

I couldn't really blame him for feeling this way. He'd been breeding a whole new strain of bacteria on that foot and I'd ruined everything. Worse still, he now had feet that didn't match. It could take years for the clean one to catch up.

"Wait," I said.

I stopped walking backward. Angie stopped too, five paces behind. And Pete, five paces behind her. I whipped out a pen and scrap of paper. These are the words I wrote.

I'm going to roll in Mom's heather till the underpants are dead. Don't say a word.

I carried the note back to Angie. Her lip trembled but she stood her ground and took it from me. "Give it to Pete," I said, and went back to my place.

Angie took the note to Pete, then returned to her place five paces in front of him. Pete read the note. He looked up. His eyes glittered. With a snarl he said, so loud that every pair of underpants this side of the moon could hear:

*"YOU'RE GOING TO ROLL IN THE HEATHER TILL YOUR UNDERPANTS ARE **DEAD**?"*

I slapped my forehead. My minutes were numbered. Now I'd *really* be made to suffer. I clung to a lamppost waiting for my life to shatter into fragments Pete could kick into the gutter.

But nothing happened.

Not a thing, apart from a little flutter around my groin.

"They've probably got a hangover after making you pig out on Pete's filthy foot," said Ange.

"You reckon?" I said hopefully.

"Either that," my ex-friend Pete said, "or they've got something even worse in store for you and are saving their strength."

I kicked up my heels and headed for home at speed.

Reaching the back gate I ran up the path, slipped the key out of the gnome's bottom, flung open the door, threw my schoolbag across the kitchen, kicked my shoes off, and removed my trousers.

I was ready.

As I strolled out to the patio I thought of the stab of pleasure I'd got when I had the idea of ordering Ryan to mop up Pete's foot. All right, it hadn't worked, my pants had turned on me, but I'd got the same bang out of telling him to do it as when I told him to eat weed. Angie had said that was pure evil. She was right. Neville the Devil was making me wicked through my underpants. I was becoming Jiggy McHyde. Also, if the Little Devils felt like a spot of extra entertainment they could make me do any of the stuff I ordered others to do. As I never knew what was going to come out of my mouth from one moment to the next, this was terrifying. The Killer Underpants had to be thwarted. Right away.

With a firm jaw and determined air, I crossed the patio in my underpants. I grinned mercilessly as I approached the heather patch in the garden. The grin still hung there for a while after I noticed something I'd missed when I ran up the path to the back door.

The heather was gone!

Janet Overton next door must have heard my groan because her head suddenly appeared on top of the fence.

"Hello, Jiggy. Tell your mom I removed the heather as she asked in her note. Give her my sympathy. I once had an allergy to butter beans."

I stood staring at the bare patch of earth that was no longer chock-a-block with the stuff that was going to solve everything.

"Butter beans?" I said.

"Used to make me break out in hives. You like those pants, don't you?"

Her head disappeared just in time. Another second and the gnome with the personalized keyhole would have flown through the air and knocked it off the fence.

Next morning I left our house just as Pete and Angie left theirs. I was about to cross the road when Pete said, "Keep away from me, McCue!"

I stopped on the curb. "Hey, be reasonable. I wasn't responsible for my own actions."

"And that's changed overnight?" he said.

Suddenly there was this loud hammering like a fist banging on wood. I glanced around. It was a fist banging on wood. The fist belonged to one of the two large men with briefcases on Pearl & Dean's front porch. The wood belonged to their door.

"The bell should work," I said to them. "It's new."

The man with the fist looked at the dinky little plastic doorbell, then he looked at his fist as if thinking, But what's the point of a fist if you can't bang on things with it? He ignored my suggestion and banged again.

My eye caught something glinting in the curtainless window above. The morning sun on Dean's shaved head. Then I saw Pearl's frizzy ginger mop. It was only the third time I'd seen Pearl. She didn't seem to go out much, not to the places I went anyway, like school. I waved to them. Dean raised a hand, then he and Pearl retreated into the shadows.

"Jiggy, go on now, you'll be late for school!"

My mother stood in the doorway in her white bathrobe. She'd come out to see what all the banging was about and was using me as an excuse.

"I'm going, I'm going."

"See you on Monday," she said, stepping out where the whole estate could see her and clasping me to her for another farewell hug.

"Mom, we've done this, go inside, you're embarrassing me."

She'd been all fond and huggy since I got up because by the time I came home from school she'd be in Paris doing the cancan alone. After work yesterday she'd spent a couple of hours with Francine, her French teacher, getting a final lingo boost. She was pretty full of herself because Francine had told her that she was her best student. Dad wasn't too thrilled about the Paris weekend. He kept warning Mom against going, ragging on the French and all, but she was so happy to be going that she just laughed in his face.

I shook my mother off and crossed the road. Angie kept her cool pretty well when I joined them, but Pete changed sides to put her between us. We stretched our necks backward as we walked away to keep in touch with what was happening at Pearl & Dean's. The two large men with briefcases were both hammering the door now and telling it to open up. I was glad I wasn't in their shoes, and not because they were so big either. On the other side of the door Chico, Harpo, and Groucho, P & D's dogs, sounded like they couldn't wait to meet them.

"Wonder what that's all about?" I said.

"Debt collectors," said Angie.

"You don't know that."

"It's the way they dress, the bags they carry, the shape of their fists. Didn't you see enough of them on Borderline Way? They even came to your house once."

"That was a mistake. Dad forgot to pay the rent."

"For a *year*?" said Pete.

English was the first period of the day. The class crashed into the English room, backpacks hit the ceiling, chairs and desks were scraped mercilessly to announce our arrival, a couple of fights broke out, and Mrs. Gamble stood there smiling sweetly, arms folded, till we simmered down and I stuck my hand up.

"Mrs. Gamble, would you punish me for something I didn't do?"

"No, Jiggy, of course not."

"Good, because I didn't do my homework."

This got a laugh, even from Mrs. Gamble, because she likes me and I'm pretty cool at English. But I couldn't relax, even here. The Big Itch could come anytime and something I said could send someone on the rampage— maybe even me, if Neville the Devil's underpants still wanted to teach me a lesson.

I stayed nervous all morning and all through lunch on my own in the Concrete Garden, abandoned by two lily-livered Musketeers and forced to eat sardine-and-tomato sandwiches and ostrich-flavor chips. To tell you the truth I felt quite lonely. Even the goldfish wouldn't meet my eye.

I went on being nervous all through history, but still no Itch. I felt sure that the Little Devils were saving themselves for something. Biding their time before making me jump headfirst in the dumpster a second before a garbage truck came along and dropped a full load of bacon rinds, eggshells, baked beans, milk cartons, and used diapers.

By the time we were in math—last lesson of the week, yippee—I was hardly daring to hope, hardly breathing. My eye was on the clock, along with a fly. Tick-tick-tick. Tock-tock-tock. I'd almost made it. Could my luck really hold for ten more minutes till the bell went? The little hand flicked to the next minute.

And it started. The ripple in the dungeon under the stairs. The warning of Things to Come.

Now nine minutes is only nine minutes to most people, but our math teacher, Face-Ache Dakin, likes to squeeze every last second out of his precious hours with us, so he didn't give a cheerful devil-may-care grin when my right arm shot out of its socket and I started yelling that I had to go to the toilet without delay. He also didn't appreciate it when Pete clapped his hands over his ears and disappeared under his desk, and was probably still trying to decide which of us to crucify first when I jumped up, leapt at the door, opened it, and fled. I heard Face-Ache screaming at me to come back at once, but I couldn't do that and I didn't have time to explain, and he wouldn't have believed me anyway.

Once out in the corridor I decided to skip the bogatorium and hoof it home. Dakin was already going to kill me for leaving his class without permission, so there was nothing to lose.

"Where do you think you're going, McCue?!"

Mr. Rice stood just outside the main office, where he'd probably been running through his athletic poses for Ms. Weeks. I didn't answer. Didn't dare. Dark forces were tickling my tonsils, trying to make me say the first thing that came into my head so someone could be made to suffer.

As I hurtled out of the school gates, spinning and twisting and scratching myself stupid, I tugged out a roll of masking tape I'd been carrying around all day for emergencies. I tore a strip off, slapped it over my mouth, headed down the street.

"McCue! Get back here this minute!"

I glanced back. Rice was coming after me. The poor red fool didn't know what he was risking. His legs were three times longer than mine and in two minutes he'd be tearing the tape off my mouth, and when my mouth started flapping . . .

I approached the shopping center all set to break the land-speed-scratching record. I ran across the square, heading for home, where I would lock myself out of harm's way and never come out again until my pants rotted. I was almost through the square when I noticed a sign over a shop with a big front window:

HEATHERS

A shop that sold heather! A flower shop! The antidote was at hand! I veered toward the shop.

"McCue! Stop right there or you—are—in—TROUBLE!"

I checked the view over my shoulder. Mr. Rice was coming up fast. I flung back the flower shop door. I ran in, scratching. There was a little woman inside, arranging flowers. I didn't dare take the tape off in case the Killer Underpants made me say something everyone would regret. I tried asking for heather by telepathic communication and grunts. Unfortunately the little woman hadn't done an evening course in telepathy and grunting and instead of giving me a bunch of heather she shrieked, threw herself back against the wall, and knocked over two flower displays, one with each hand. The flower displays toppled sideways, one one way, the other the other. Then each of them hit another, which hit another, and suddenly displays were tumbling all around the shop like falling dominoes but more color- ful. The terrified owner fled into a little office at the back and shoved a bolt across the door. I had no choice then. I had to help myself. I looked around, scratching frantically. Heather . . . heather . . . where? There wasn't any. Not the tiniest bit. And then I realized.

Heather must be the name of the woman who owned the shop!

Suddenly the world crashed. I turned. The big win- dow had been struck by a tumbling display case. It was imploding in a krillion pieces. And the door beside it was opening. Mr. Rice was coming in, forehead throb- bing. He was reaching for me with two enormous claws. And as he reached, the itching started to run out of steam. Ten seconds and I'd be back to normal, and in BIIIIIG trouble.

Unless . . .

I barely noticed the pain as I ripped the masking tape off my mouth.

"Pay for all the damage and forget you saw me today!" I screamed at Mr. Rice.

His great hams dropped to his sides. Then one of them unzipped the little money pouch he wore around his waist and took out a credit card. I looked him in the eye. It looked away. I looked him in the other eye. It also looked away. I'd told him to forget he'd seen me today, and he *couldn't see me!* I stepped past him. He was knocking on the office door, eager to hand his credit card to Heather, the owner.

I went home, pleased that the Killer Underpants hadn't turned the tables on me again. If they'd made me do what I told Rice to—pay for the broken glass and all—I'd still be handing over my allowance when I was eighty.

18

Saturday again. Blessed Saturday. I phoned Pete and Angie and talked them into coming to the market with me for moral support. I had to have another go at persuading Neville the Devil to free me from the curse of the underpants before I started World War III.

"What about Pearl & Dean then?" Angie said on the way.

"Yeah, shame," I said.

"I always knew there was something about them," Pete said from somewhere behind. He still wasn't too eager to be near me.

"First time you've mentioned it," said Angie.

"Yeah, well," said Pete. "I always knew."

What happened about Pearl & Dean was this. The two men with briefcases who'd hammered at their door and demanded to be let in were bailiffs come to turf them out. The reason they wanted to do this was that P & D didn't own the house, didn't pay any kind of mortgage or rent, didn't have any right to be there whatsoever. They were squatters. Which explained the curtain famine.

"I'll miss Dean," I said. "So will my dad. Now his football team will be outnumbered."

It was still quite early by the time we got to the market, so it wasn't exactly milling with people. I led the way to the red stall with gold stars. Instead of clothing it had kitcheny stuff today, like Neville said it would, and every saucepan, cheese grater, can opener, knife and fork and spoon had a small logo that read *Little Devils*.

"Hey," Neville said, laying the Bad Grin on me, "the ungrateful kid with the lucky underpants."

"Excuse me?" I said. "Lucky? Have you any idea what these things have put me through this week?"

"Sure. I know a lotta stuff. Devils do." He leaned toward me, very close. "This is only the beginning, kid. A month from now you could be famous. Locked up with the key thrown away, but famous. Think of it."

My future life flashed past my eyes. I wasn't going to enjoy it. Angie stepped forward. "Listen," she said with a growl that I'd have to clone for my own use at the earliest opportunity, "my friend's underpants are making his life a misery—"

"And mine," said Pete, standing firmly behind her.

"—and whatever it is you put in them has got to be removed before something goes seriously wrong—right? Now are you going to do it or are we going to have to take this further?"

Neville heard her out. Then he adjusted his little red bowler hat and gave her the Grin. "Further?" he said. "Like where exactly?"

"Where?" said Angie.

"Where you gonna take it? What are you gonna do about it?"

Angie groped for an answer, but none came. I took charge again.

"Look . . . sir . . . all I want is to get my underpants off. You needn't worry, I won't tell a soul about them. You can sell as many pairs as you like. You can outfit the entire civilized world with them, just set me free, release me, that's all I ask."

"How selfish can you get?" Pete said from the back.

"I'm desperate," I snapped. "What do you say?" I said to Neville.

"I say learn to live with them," said he. "I say go out

into the world and make mischief. I say bring a little joy to the jolly black heart of Neville the Devil."

Angie jumped in again. "Neville the Devil! Lucifer's kid brother! What do you take us for? You're a phony. Just another market trader selling gimmicky junk, and I'm warning you . . ."

Her voice trailed off. It trailed off because Neville had removed his hat and we were staring at the two little warty stumps on the head underneath.

Little warty stumps that began to grow before our eyes.

That developed points.

That became horns.

Pete and Angie and I took turns to look at one another. When we'd seen enough, we nodded, spun around, and ran like heck.

They got farther than I did because they didn't crash into a little old lady with a basket on her arm. I gripped the old dame's scrawny elbows to stop her from tumbling into the crowd and being trampled to skin and bone. She smiled gummily up at me.

"Lucky heather?" she croaked, shoving her basket in my face.

I sniffed the purple stuff suddenly decorating my nostrils. "Huh?"

"Hey, you! Crone! Geddaway from here, I told you last week!"

Neville the Devil sounded upset. I glanced back just in time to see him plonk his hat on the two small puffs of smoke that hovered where his horns had been. Then I saw why he was miffed. His shiny saucepans and strainers and can openers and knives and forks and spoons had gone dull. All of them. Some were actually turning black. The prongs on the forks were starting to wither and curl up.

"Must be the heather," muttered Ange, who'd come back when she caught me missing.

"Yeah . . ." I said, feasting my eyes.

And the lucky gypsy heather wasn't only getting to the stuff on the stall either. I felt a definite sag in the cargo hold. I gave a little wriggle, rearranged the personal equipment.

Pete had also returned by this time, and the three of us stood gawping at the stall, which didn't seem anything like as red as it had been—more a pinky gray, with the gold stars turning to tarnished brass. Even Neville's clothes weren't as bright as they had been, and the man himself had gone quite pale. He was still telling the gypsy woman to get lost, but in a much smaller, weaker, almost pleading voice.

"Dracula," said Pete.

"Eh?" I said.

"What happens when the ancient professor type holds a crucifix in front of Drac's eyes?"

"He goes a bit off-color," Angie said.

"He goes a lot off-color," said Pete.

"He's not too fond of garlic either," I reminded them.

"Nor am I," said Ange, "but I don't curl up and die."

"I'm talking heather here," Pete said impatiently. "Like heather and Neville the Devil? With me so far?"

"Hey," I said.

"Exactly," said Pete.

I spun on the old gypsy lady. "How much for the lot?"

"Make me an offer I can't refuse," she replied, suddenly a smart-aleck Mafia person in a shawl.

I went through my pockets and held my palm out to show her my personal fortune before tax.

"I can refuse that," she said, and spat on my shoes.

"Angie," I said, "Pete. Give me your money! All of it!"

"Get outta here," said Pete.

"This is an emergency," I said.

"Your emergency, not mine."

I snatched his chest, did a Rice on him, forehead to forehead, nose to nose, tried to make the veins stand out in my neck.

"Gimme your spondulicks or next time I get the Itch I send out a hit squad, and that's a promise."

He smirked but turned his pockets out. While he was doing this I asked the little old gypsy how the Eye was. She said it was fine, thanks for asking. I showed her our combined wealth.

"Help yourselves," she said, snatching the cash.

I whipped my shirt out, loosened my belt, shoved a sprig of heather inside the band of the underpants (which were loose, loose, loose). "Ouch!" I said, and raised the sprig a smidgen.

Then the three of us each grabbed two big handfuls of heather from the basket and advanced on the stall, holding the heather before us like purple torches. The closer we got, the more the kitcheny stuff withered and twisted and darkened. And as for Neville . . .

Neville the Devil started to shrivel before our eyes—hat and vest and all. "You can't do this to me," he said as he shrank. We leaned over the stall, waving heather. He glared up at us, but he was no longer big enough to be scary. First he became a very small Neville, then a tiny Neville, then an itsy-witsy Neville. His foot slipped on something, and he went shooting into a drain, cute little hands clutching wildly. He got a grip on the grille, and hung from it. "I'm sorry," Angie said, "but you have to go," and dropped some heather on his hands. This must have caused Neville's grip to weaken, for when he next spoke his voice faded away to nothing.

"I'll be baaaaaaaaaaaaaaaack ..."

A few people had gathered around. We'd been blocking the view, so they hadn't seen Neville shrink to Barbie's Ken size and go down the drain. They could see the stuff on the stall though. The withered, twisted, superdull kitcheny stuff. And was it their imagination? Hadn't this sad gray sagging stall been bright red when they last looked? And those grubby little blobs all over it, hadn't they been . . . gold stars?

"Oh *there* you are, Mother!" a familiar voice said nearby. "I've been looking for you everywhere. Is this disappearing act going to be a regular Saturday market thing? And where's that heather you keep buying from the flower shop? Don't tell me you've sold it all again."

Pete was quickest off the mark. He jumped into the crowd and found some shoulders to peer over. Angie and I followed his example. From there, the three of us watched Ms. Erica Weeks, vice principal of Ranting

Lane School, chat to her mother, the little old woman who bought heather from the flower shop when it came in on Saturdays and sold it on to dupes like me for all the money their friends had in the world.

19

Rushing home from the market with heather stuffed down my pants, I went straight upstairs, slammed my bedroom door, put a chair against it, and breathed deeply. They dropped as easy as pie. Slithered all the way to the carpet without a murmur of complaint, or even a parting squeeze. A lump rose in my throat. I'd begun to wonder if I'd ever see underpants around my ankles again. I was so happy I stepped out of them and did a jig of joy around the room, whirling them around my head, singing at the top of my voice. This might have gone on for some time if I hadn't noticed the window cleaner grinning like teeth had just been invented. He raised both thumbs at me (bad move on a ladder) and lost his footing. Must have banged his chin on twelve or thirteen rungs before he hit my mother's poor old rock garden.

. . .

Mom came back early from Paris. A day and a half early actually, that night, as Dad and I were scoffing pizza and fries, feet on the coffee table, horror film from the video store on TV. Suddenly she's standing in the doorway watching this crazed werewolf tear this innocent hitchhiker apart.

"Mom! What are you doing here?"

In one swift movement Dad shoved the last of his fries down his throat, stopped the video, removed his feet from the table, and stood up to accept the Perfect Husband of the Year Award to a round of silent applause. Then he asked Mom why she wasn't in Paris. She didn't exactly answer, just said she was never going there again, which made Dad go all smug, though he tried not to show it.

"Rude were they, the French?" he said.

Mom grunted tragically.

Dad put an arm around her so he could wipe his greasy fingers on her shoulder. "So what do they know?"

Mom shrugged him off. "They know how French *should* sound."

"Well, so do you. You should, you've been learning it since 1776."

"Yes!" she screeched, and ran to the door. *"With a Brooklyn accent!"*

I was leaving the bathroom the next morning when my mother shot out of my room with the ex-Killer Underpants dangling from the end of my Kings and Queens of Sweden ruler.

"What were these revolting things doing on your lampshade?"

"Revolting?" I said. "I thought you liked them."

I didn't dare tell her that her eyes were as red as sun-dried tomatoes and her face twice its normal size. I'd have to wait till she was staring in horror at the mirror to smuggle out all the lucky heather I'd stuffed under my bed last night.

Mom wouldn't allow any other dirty clothes in the washing machine with the underpants, but that suited me fine. Gave me the opportunity to sit in front of it shouting, "Take that! And that! And that!" every time they thudded over in the foam. Most fun I'd had all week. Pete and Angie spoiled things by coming over before the washing cycle finished. When I opened the door I thought they must have been to a special Sunday clinic to give blood, because there wasn't any in their faces.

"Have you seen?" Angie said.

"Seen what?" I said.

"Have you *seen*?" Pete said.

"Seen *what*?" I said.

They stood back to give me a clear view of the street. A big battered old van stood on the pavement outside the empty house next door. Men were unloading things and carrying them in. One of the men was Mr. Atkins. The other was his tattooed son Jolyon.

I was up in my room that afternoon doing some homework I'd managed to hide from myself all week when some sixth or seventh sense made me go to the window. Coming across the back fence that separates us from our new neighbors was a long pole with a butcher's hook on the end. The hook was heading for the line of clothes Mom had spent the day washing instead of talking Brooklyn French in Paris. Reaching the line, the hook found the item it wanted, tugged a couple of times, and carried my sparkling clean Little Devils back across the fence.

I was puzzled. What sane person would want to steal the things? But then I remembered Eejit Atkins and last Monday's showers after soccer when he said he thought my briefs were cool and I said he could have them if I ever got them off. Well, a promise is a promise. Besides, my mother had worn out her best scrubbing brush on them before turning them over to the washing machine to be pummeled to death. Nothing could survive treatment like that. The worst damage Atkins could do with them was blind everyone when he took off his pants in the changing rooms. "Bye-bye, Killer Underpants!" I chortled merrily, and returned to my homework.

You won't be surprised to hear that my mother refused to believe I wasn't behind the Little Devils' disappearance. But I could live with that. I could live with anything now. I was smiling again. I was even smiling as I left the house for school on Monday morning. Pete and Angie greeted me just like the old days. Pete put his arm around my neck and squeezed. "I hope you appreciate how I stood by you," he said.

I knocked his brand-new booster shot scab off.

"One for all and all for lunch," said Angie, and we did the secret handshake I'm not going to tell you about, and headed schoolward with a jolly air and a spring in our step. Everything was back to normal.

"Ay, wait up!"

Eejit Atkins ran out of the house where Pearl & Dean had squatted happily with Chico, Harpo, and Groucho, and loped after us.

"Great, isn't it?" he said out of the side of his mouth. "We're neighbors agin. We can go to school together every day!"

"Yeah that's really great, Atkins," I said out of the side of my mouth.

"Dream come true," said Pete out of the side of his mouth.

"Happiest day of my life," said Angie out of the side of her mouth.

"Hey," Atkins said as we left the estate, "I could be the other Muskiteer, couldn't I?"

"What other Muskiteer?" I asked.

"That Dartanyanyan guy. The one that buys it at the end."

"Pick those feet up, you all!" cried the hearty voice of something in red as it jogged past.

"This I do not believe," said Pete.

Nor did I. Nor did Angie. Mr. Rice was not alone. There was another track-suited type with him. He'd found a jogging partner. A vice principal jogging partner.

"Ooh!" said Eejit Atkins.

"You never said a truer word, Atkins," said Pete.

But Eejit hadn't oohed because of Rice and his fellow jogger. No, it was something else. He gave a little wiggle as he walked. Then a bigger wiggle. Then his hips went all peculiar and he fell to the ground, rolled off the curb kicking air.

And scratching. Like a maniac.

"That's not what I used to do, is it?" I said.

"Yeah," said Pete.

"Exactly what you used to do," said Ange.

"You know what this means, don't you?" I said. "It means the Killer Underpants aren't dead. It means all they needed was a rest from heather and wash day. It means we'd better ruuuuuuun!!!"

Six Musketeer feet hit the pavement. Sparks flew.

"Hey, you three!" Eejit Atkins shouted from the gutter.

We covered our ears, stared straight ahead like runaway horses with nails in their tails. Mr. Rice and Ms. Weeks gaped as we galloped past. So did everyone else. They'd never seen kids in such a hurry to get to school. Certainly not this kid.

JiGGY McCUE